"Oh, no, Mr. Kyle, you are mistaken!"

Sara raised her head with a touch of pride. "I've no intention of coming to live at Malthorpe. And don't try your boardroom tactics on me, they just won't work."

"Boardroom tactics—" Jarrod said, amused. "You haven't the slightest idea what they are."

"Well, maybe not," she said hotly. "But you can't make me do anything!"

"Ah, well, Miss Robins," he said smoothly. "There you are wrong. However unpleasant you may find the news, I am your guardian and as such, I have absolute power over you."

"But why?" Sara protested. "Only last week you were suggesting I was using your father as a meal ticket."

"I know—and my opinion hasn't changed. But my father is insistent," he went on. "So let's not waste any more time!"

ANNE MATHER

moon witch

Harlequin Books

TORONTO · LONDON · LOS ANGELES · AMSTERDAM
SYDNEY · HAMBURG · PARIS · STOCKHOLM · ATHENS · TOKYO

Harlequin Presents edition published March 1974
ISBN 0-373-15039-3

Second printing May 1974
Third printing July 1974
Fourth printing August 1974
Fifth printing February 1977
Sixth printing March 1977
Seventh printing May 1977
Eighth printing December 1978
Ninth printing April 1982

Original hardcover edition published in 1970
by Mills & Boon Limited

CHAPTER ONE

THE pretty stewardess came down the aisle of the Super VC 10, and stopped beside the seat of one of her first-class passengers. 'We'll be landing in fifteen minutes, Mr. Kyle,' she said, smiling politely.

The man looked up from the file of papers he had been studying with deep concentration, frowning slightly at the interruption. 'What? Oh yes, fifteen minutes, thank you.' He nodded briefly, and returned to his papers, and the stewardess gave an almost imperceptible lift of her shoulders before returning to her position at the rear of the plane. She looked resentfully at her fellow-stewardess and said:

'Honestly, I don't know when I've ever been so disappointed!'

The other girl smiled questioningly. 'Why?'

'Well, having Jarrod Kyle as a passenger, of course. Heavens, the reputation he has I thought he'd at least notice me! As it is, I don't think he sees me as anything more than part of the fuselage!'

The other girl laughed. 'And is he attractive?'

The stewardess shrugged. 'Not particularly. In fact he's quite unattractive. He has one of those hard, craggy faces; I'm sure his nose has been broken. He's big, of course, and having hair of that silvery shade is unusual, I suppose, but he's very thin!'

'Poor Mr. Kyle,' said the other girl, still amused.

5

'You're certainly exploding the myth. Which one is he?'

'I'll show you, as they leave,' replied the stewardess tartly, and returned to her duties.

Jarrod Kyle was surprised when the huge airliner landed at London Airport to find both stewardesses appraising him thoroughly. Turning his blue eyes on them, he said: 'Say, is anything wrong? Did I snore in my sleep or something?'

Both girls gave embarrassed smiles, and one of them said: 'I hope you enjoyed the flight, Mr. Kyle.'

Nodding, he shrugged his broad shoulders and walked down the catwalk into the airport buildings. As he disappeared, one of the girls looked exasperatedly at the other. 'Did you say he *wasn't* attractive!' she exclaimed.

Meanwhile, Jarrod Kyle was given V.I.P. clearance of Customs and carrying his briefcase, his overcoat slung over one shoulder, he crossed the reception hall to where John Matthews, his personal assistant, was waiting for him. 'Hi, Matt,' he said warmly.

'Good to see you, Jarrod. Did you have a good holiday?' responded Matt, grinning.

'Fine,' Jarrod nodded, falling into step beside the other man. 'Plenty of fishing—the way I like it.'

'Catch anything?' Matt glanced his way.

'Depends what you mean,' remarked Jarrod dryly. 'How's the old man?'

'J.K.? Oh, he's okay, I guess. Are you driving up there tonight?'

Jarrod glanced at his watch. 'I guess so. It's after five-thirty—let's go have a drink and you can tell

6

me what's been happening.'

Matt looked at him thoughtfully. 'I think that would be a good idea, Jarrod,' he agreed mildly, pushing open the door of the bar.

Over whisky on the rocks, the way Jarrod liked it, Matt said: 'There's been quite an unexpected bombshell, actually. Want to hear about it?'

Jarrod lit a cigar. 'Of course,' he said, his eyes narrowing. 'Not the Bradford merger?'

'No,' Matt shook his head. 'That deal went through all right. J.K. handled it himself. I guess he thought he ought to pick up the reins in your absence, so to speak. I don't think he'll ever completely retire, do you?'

Jarrod took his cigar out and studied the glowing tip. 'So? What's this bombshell? Don't keep me in suspense, Matt.'

Matt swallowed a mouthful of whisky before replying. 'You might find it amusing,' he said. 'You seem to have got yourself a ward, unless your solicitors can extract you from the involvement, which, knowing them, I guess they will.'

Jarrod stared at him curiously. 'A ward? What the hell are you talking about? A ward!' he looked exasperated. 'What kind of ward? A hospital ward? A political thing? What?'

'No, Jarrod, nothing like that! A ward—a kid, you know!'

'You mean like I've been made guardian to some kid?' Jarrod looked astounded.

'Something like that!' Matt grinned. 'Quaint, isn't it?'

Jarrod swallowed his whisky at a gulp, and ordered another. 'I don't know what in hell you're talking about, Matt. Come on, let's have it. From the top!'

Matt twisted his glass round in his fingers. 'It's quite simple, really, Jarrod. Some old guy has made you his granddaughter's guardian, till she's twenty-one. Or eighteen, maybe. I'm not too sure about that.'

Jarrod was growing impatient. 'What old guy?' he asked shortly.

Matt looked amused. 'A man called Jeffrey Robins. He died a couple of weeks ago.'

'Jeffrey Robins!' Jarrod looked blank. 'Do I know him—or should I say—did I know him?'

Matt shook his head. 'Unlikely,' he replied, 'he was a foreman in the Bridchester warehouse for forty years before he died.'

Jarrod breathed down his nose hard. 'Matt, I'm warning you——'

Matt laughed. 'Hold it, Jarrod, don't blame me! It's not my pigeon. Your father knows all about it. He used to know Jeffrey Robins.'

'At last! The first bit of information. How did my father know him?'

'Well, I believe they began in the textile trade together, years ago, but when J.K. left to start his own company, they lost touch. Then in the war they met again, and I believe it was during the early fifties when your father moved the head office to London they lost touch again.'

'I still don't understand, Matt. If J.K. knew him so well, why didn't he make my father this kid's guardian? And where are her own parents, anyway?'

Matt accepted his second whisky. 'Well, it's like this, you see, Jarrod, old man Robins made the chairman of Kyle Textiles his granddaughter's guardian. He wasn't to know your father would have to retire and give the chairmanship over to you when he was only fifty-eight.'

Jarrod stubbed out his cigar savagely. 'My God!' he said, shaking his head. 'That was eight years ago!'

'Yes, well, like I said, he was out of touch. I don't suppose he expected to die so suddenly—after all, he was only sixty-eight himself.'

'I see.' Jarrod thrust his arms into the sleeves of his overcoat. 'What a goddamned situation! And what about this kid's parents? Where are they?'

'Her mother died in childbirth, and the father got himself killed in an earthquake in South America. He worked for an insurance agency or something.'

'Ah!' Jarrod nodded, chewing his lip thoughtfully. 'Oh well, come on, Matt. You can tell me more on our way to town.'

Outside the warm brilliance of the airport buildings a chilly fog had descended, making a damp January evening even more dismal. Jarrod turned up the collar of his coat, and glanced cheerfully at Matt. 'I guess I should have stayed away longer. Who in hell would want to come back to London from Jamaica at this time of the year? I must be crazy!'

Matt allowed Jarrod to slide behind the wheel of the huge Mercedes that awaited them. 'You know fine you can't keep away,' he remarked dryly. 'It's in your blood: high finance, boardrooms, mergers, take-overs; you name it, you can do it!'

Jarrod shrugged, turning the car expertly on to

9

the main thoroughfare. 'You make me sound like a machine,' he remarked wryly.

Matt grinned, glancing out of the windows at the heavy gloom, illuminated by the orange glow of fog-lamps. 'You're far from that, Jarrod, thank God!' he said, with enthusiasm. 'Sometimes your father would say—too far!'

Jarrod gave a short laugh. 'Jealousy, that's all, Matt. The old man was never able to settle for a quiet life. He'd love to have been born thirty years later.'

Matt laughed now. 'Oh yes, one of the jet set, eh? Dolly birds, fast cars, the *dolce vita*!'

'Something like that,' agreed Jarrod, pressing his foot down on the accelerator. 'Tell me about the child now. What is she like?'

Matt shook his head. 'I've no idea. I haven't seen her. I only know she's still at school.'

Jarrod raised his eyes heavenward. 'And what does the old man say we do?'

'I think he's waiting for you to come home to discuss it. He wanted to bring you back sooner, but I persuaded him you needed a holiday.'

'Thanks,' said Jarrod dryly. 'That's what I was wondering about. It's not like J.K. to hold back on me. He doesn't usually pull his punches.'

'No, well, anyway, you'll hear all about it soon enough. He expects you to drive up to Malthorpe tonight.'

'Does he? Yes, well, maybe I'll take a rain check on that,' said Jarrod, swinging round a jay-walking pedestrian.

'Do you think you should? You know—his blood-pressure——'

10

'All right, all right,' muttered Jarrod impatiently. 'All right, Matt, we'll just call at the apartment and leave my things for Hastings. What a life! Six weeks in Jamaica, and within an hour of arriving back in this country I feel as though I've never been away.'

Malthorpe in the Forest was in Yorkshire, a comfortable village not far from the textile mills of Leeds and Bradford where the Kyle empire had had its source. Now, with factories in most of the larger countries of the world, it was an international organisation whose head office was in London. Jarrod's father had founded the business before the Second World War and even he had had no idea of the impact his materials, carpets and designs would have on the rest of the world.

Jarrod and Matt arrived at the outskirts of Malthorpe late in the evening of the same day. J.K., as Jarrod's father was always called, liked the kind of country squireship he had assumed upon buying the old country home of the Malthorpe family, all of whom were now only remembered by the gravestones in the cemetery beside the village church. Malthorpe Hall was large and sprawling, without much elegance of design outside. Its part-Georgian façade had been added to by succeeding generations without much discrimination and in consequence it now belonged to no period. Inside, Jarrod's father had installed every kind of modern convenience. The large rooms suited his expansive personality, and he had spared nothing to make it the most talked about house in the district, much envied and admired by his friends and acquaintances. It stood in thickly wooded grounds, which stretched for some

11

distance across the fields that gave on to the open moors. A high fence prevented would-be sightseers from getting too close, and as Jarrod approached its entrance he was forced to stop and identify himself to Hedley, the lodge-keeper.

'Well, we're in,' he remarked dryly to Matt, as the car sped up the dark tree-lined drive. 'It gets a little more like Fort Knox every time I come!'

'Your father is afraid someone will steal his precious antiques,' said Matt, as Jarrod brought the car to a halt in the gravelled courtyard before the front doors. 'And every new piece he gets adds to his collection.'

'And to his nerves,' said Jarrod, sliding out of the car. 'God, it's cold! Have you had any snow yet?'

'No, not yet. And it's not that cold, Jarrod. It's not even freezing, or you wouldn't have been able to go as fast as you did on the motorway.'

'Want a bet?' asked Jarrod, mockingly, as the doors opened and light flooded out on to them. 'Hello, Morris. On cue as ever!'

The uniformed butler bowed politely. 'Good evening, Mr. Jarrod. I trust you've had a good journey.'

Jarrod nodded, walking round to the rear of the Mercedes and opening the boot. 'Fine. How's my father?' He extracted his cases easily.

Morris came forward and took the cases from him firmly. 'Your father is quite well, Mr. Jarrod. He is waiting for you in the library. Will you be wanting any supper, sir?'

Jarrod mounted the steps followed closely by Matt, carrying his briefcase and overcoat. 'No, thanks, not tonight. See you later, Matt.'

Matt nodded and turned to follow Morris up the stairs to the first landing. Jarrod crossed the wide hall, and entered a room on the far side. The hall was lit by an exquisite crystal chandelier and Jarrod heard the prisms tinkling slightly in the sudden draught from the front door. The hall was carpeted in dark blue and gold, the balustrade of the staircase echoing the gold in filigree work overlaying the mellowed panelling which Jarrod's father had retained. The library which he entered was carpeted in dark green, its walls lined with hundreds of hidebound books that Jarrod was sure his father had never even opened. J.K. was not a scholarly man, his success had been due to his hard work and personality, and he was not content to sit back and let someone else handle all the action. Unfortunately, a severe heart attack eight years ago had convinced him that to carry on living at the rate he was doing would kill him inside a year, so he had handed over the chairmanship of the Kyle companies to his son Jarrod, with the intention of retaining an active role in its administration. However, he had acted without thought to Jarrod's own part in the proceedings, and found that his son could be as obstinate as he was. Thus, Jarrod took complete control of the business, only consulting his father rarely, much, to J.K.'s chagrin. Now, though, he found he admired his son immensely, and what he had done was no less than he would have done in his place.

Tonight J.K. was sitting beside a roaring fire, smoking a cigar and drinking some superlative cognac from a balloon glass as his son entered. Although the whole house was centrally heated, J.K. insisted that he retained the fire in the library. He

13

looked up as Jarrod entered, and smiled warmly.

'Well, hello, Jarrod,' he said, nodding to the chair opposite him. 'Come and sit down! Is it freezing outside?'

'Not according to Matt,' remarked Jarrod, pouring himself some brandy and taking the seat his father indicated. 'But it's bloody cold!'

J.K. laughed. 'You've grown soft, out there in the Caribbean. Don't know how you stand the heat myself. Give me a crisp autumn day and a good fire, and I'm content.'

'You're getting old, J.K.,' said Jarrod deliberately, and laughed when his father looked annoyed. 'Say, but let's not waste time on trivialities; what's all this about some kid I'm guardian to?'

J.K. drew on his cigar, nodding. 'Yes, Sara Robins. Old Jeff's granddaughter!'

'But this is crazy, isn't it?' Jarrod looked impatient, running a hand through the silvery hair which grew low on the back of his neck. 'Hell, how did he come to make you his granddaughter's guardian?'

'Not me, *you*!' said J.K. with some satisfaction. 'You, Jarrod! The chairman of Kyle Textiles!'

'That's only a formality,' muttered Jarrod, chewing his cigar. 'You know damn fine it was you, and not me, he was talking about. Anyway, you still haven't explained.'

J.K. shrugged his broad shoulders. He was like his son; he had the same thick hair, but his was iron grey, and his features were more deeply carved. Also, his eyes were grey; Jarrod got his unusual eyes from his mother. 'When I was a young man, Jeff and I were good friends. I guess when his daughter and son-in-law both died he felt disturbed for the child's welfare. After all, his own wife died during the war, he must have felt the girl was completely alone.'

'But why pick on you? For the money?'

J.K.'s lips curled. 'If you had known Jeff Robins you wouldn't say a thing like that. He was the most honest, upstanding man I know. If he had wanted money he could have had it. I offered him plenty of chances one way and another. No, Jarrod, it must just have been a kind of hopeful desperation, I guess. I don't think he knew about his heart condition, or if he did, he didn't broadcast it. I guess he hoped to be around till Sara was old enough to find herself a man and get married.' He sighed. 'But it wasn't to be!'

'And the child, have you seen her? Since her grandfather died, I mean.'

'I've never seen her,' said his father, lying back in his chair reflectively. 'I suppose I ought to have gone over to Bridchester this past week, but I thought I'd wait——'

'And let me do it,' said Jarrod dryly. 'Clever!'

His father grinned. 'Well, Jarrod, you did insist on taking over every part of my duties. How was I to know you wouldn't object to me interfering?'

'Crafty devil!' muttered Jarrod, walking across to help himself to another drink. 'Okay, okay, what are we doing about it?' He leant against a table, looking at his father. 'Seriously!'

His father frowned. 'Well, I guess it would be an easy matter to contest the will. After all, it wouldn't be difficult to prove that it was I, and not you, who ought to be the—how shall I put it?—trustee! And as I'm now retired, I imagine that would absolve our responsibilities legally.' He rocked the liquid in his glass. 'Besides, the will was made without our consent, and I suppose that means something.'

Jarrod heaved a sigh. 'What a situation! What will happen to the kid if we do—absolve ourselves?'

'I suppose she'll be put into a foster home, or something. Unless we provide funds to keep her until she's capable of keeping herself.'

'Where is she now?'

'Staying with a neighbour, but as this neighbour has seven children of her own she's made it plain, to the solicitors at least, that it can't be a lasting arrangement.'

'Poor kid!' Jarrod swallowed the remainder of his brandy. 'Well, I suppose you expect me to go see her.'

'One of us has to,' said his father, leaning forward. 'After all, it's only the decent thing to do.'

'And then what?' Jarrod stood down his glass, and loosened the top button of his shirt. 'That's better,' he sighed. 'I guess the best thing is to provide for her, isn't it?'

His father shrugged. 'I have a fancy to see Jeff's granddaughter, Jarrod. Bring her here, to see me.'

Jarrod raised his dark eyebrows. 'Are you serious?'

'Why not?'

'Well, I mean, you're going to bring a kid here, to see—well—all this, and then put her back in her place! Don't you think it's likely to make her discontented?'

'Not if she's Jeff's granddaughter,' replied J.K. firmly. 'He'll have seen she has both feet on the ground.'

'Anyway, how old is she?' Jarrod frowned. 'You never did get round to that.'

J.K. shrugged. 'I'm not exactly sure. Fifteen or so, I think.'

'Fifteen!' Jarrod glared at him. 'Fifteen. Don't you realise that girls of fifteen are practically grown up!'

His father narrowed his eyes. 'How do you know that, Jarrod? Or are your tastes in women changing?'

Jarrod threw the end of his cigar on the fire. 'If anyone else had said that to me . . .' he said harshly.

'I know, I know.' His father rose to his feet. 'Nevertheless, you have known plenty of women, and maybe you're right. Maybe she's not a child after all. If this is the case, it would make our job easier. Unless . . .' J.K. looked thoughtful. 'I always wanted a daughter, Jarrod,' he said reflectively. 'Oh, I know I wanted a son—but afterwards——' He sighed.

Jarrod walked to the door, stretching. 'Oh, brother,' he said with some sarcasm. 'The brandy must be making you maudlin. I'm tired. I'm going to bed. Sleep on it, and let me know what you've decided in the morning.'

His father compressed his lips, looking annoyed. 'All right, Jarrod, you've made your point,' he said shortly. 'How hard you are!'

Jarrod looked back at the slightly stooped figure of his father and repented. 'I'm as you've made me, J.K.,' he said slowly. 'In your own image!'

Sara Robins walked home from school with Brian Mason, the eldest son of Mrs. Mason, who had been

17

her grandfather's neighbour for over fifteen years. It was with them that Sara was staying, while her future plans were considered. Although it was only a little over two weeks since her grandfather's death, Sara felt as though a lifetime had gone by.

The reading of the will, and the discovery that her grandfather had placed her virtually in the care of a complete stranger had come as a shock to her. If she had ever considered her grandfather's health, she had never dreamed that he might collapse before she had left school and got herself a job. Somehow he had always seemed so young, so robust, that he had never invited any anxiety about his condition. It was only now that Sara realised he must have had some warning of the heart disease he had suffered.

Mrs. Mason and her husband, who always seemed such a meek, long-suffering little man, compared to his domineering wife, had been very kind, but Sara knew that she could not stay with the Masons indefinitely. Accommodation was limited, and at the moment she was sleeping on a camp-bed in their sitting-room. The house next door had been put up for sale, but it was not expected that they would get much for it. Such furniture as had been suitable had been taken to the saleroom, and Sara averted her eyes when she passed the blank empty windows.

A huge cream car was standing at the Masons' gate this afternoon and Brian said: 'Gosh! It's a Mercedes, Sara! It must be someone from that man —that Mr. Kyle, for you!'

Sara shook her head, her mouth suddenly dry. Since the solicitors had first advised her of that clause in the will she had deliberately put all thoughts of it out of her mind. Now, seeing the cream Mercedes, it all came flooding back, and with it a frightening sense of panic.

Brian was looking at her strangely. 'What's wrong? You've gone all white, Sara! Heavens, there's nothing to be scared about. I wish it was me that was going to be involved with a man like that —as *rich* as that!'

Sara looked scornfully at him. 'Money! Is that all you can think about? I feel like a bartered object —like something at the saleroom!'

Brian laughed. 'Well, you don't look like one, Sara. Wait until he sees you. He'll probably turn out to be a real sugar-daddy!'

'You mean a dirty old man,' said Sara gloomily.

'Is he old?'

'Well, it stands to reason, he must be,' exclaimed Sara. 'He was Grandfather's contemporary!'

'Y–e–s,' said Brian slowly. 'Well, come on, let's go and see!'

They entered the narrow hall of the Masons' house. There was the low murmur of voices coming from the sitting-room, and Sara looked apprehensively at Brian. He grinned cheerfully at her, and then the sitting-room door opened and Mrs. Mason came out. When she saw Sara she quickly closed the door, and came across to her.

'Mr. Kyle's here to see you,' she whispered conspiratorially. 'At least he says he's Mr. Kyle. He's much younger than I expected, and of course, I didn't like to ask questions.'

Sara reserved her own opinion. Mrs. Mason was not the type of person not to ask questions, and it could only mean that Mr. Kyle had not appeased her by answering them.

'He's waiting to see you,' went on Mrs. Mason, as Sara did not reply. 'Do you want me to come in with you?'

Sara bit her lip. 'Er—no, I don't think so, Mrs. Mason,' she said awkwardly.

Mrs. Mason stiffened and folded her arms across her ample breast. 'Well, of course, if that's what you want, Sara,' she said reproachfully.

Sara moved her shoulders. 'I—I think it would be best, Mrs. Mason.'

'Very well. Come along, Brian.' Mrs. Mason swept off along the hall towards the kitchen, and sighing, Sara walked to the sitting-room door. Gathering up her small store of courage she opened the door, and walked in, closing it firmly behind her.

A man rose from his seat in a low armchair at her entrance. He was tall and lean, with crinkly, ash-blond hair that persisted in lying over his forehead, despite his attempts to brush it back. His face was tanned a deep brown, as though he had just spent several weeks in the sun, while he had the bluest eyes she had ever seen. He was not handsome, she thought nervously, but he was certainly no contemporary of her grandfather's.

If she was surprised at his appearance, he seemed no less surprised at hers. '*You* are Sara Robins?' he exclaimed.

Sara swallowed hard. 'Yes, Mr. Kyle. I'm Sara Robins.'

'How old are you?'

Sara shrugged. 'Um—well—seventeen, actually,' she faltered.

'Seventeen! I see.' He drew out a cigar case. 'Do you mind?' and as she shook her head, he took a cigar out and lit it. 'My—my father thought you were perhaps fifteen. Instead, you——' He halted. 'Are you planning to leave school soon?'

'I suppose I can leave when I like,' replied Sara carefully, studying her fingernails. 'When—when Grandfather was alive I did intend to go on to take "A" levels, but now . . .' Her voice trailed away.

He moved impatiently, and gave her a strange look. 'Well, Sara Robins, haven't you any questions you want to ask me?'

Sara was taken aback. 'You—you're younger than I expected.'

'Well, maybe so.' He shrugged his broad shoulders. 'Your grandfather made a slight error of judgement. He left your future in the hands of the chairman of Kyle Textiles expecting my father still to be in that position.'

'Your *father*!' Sara stared at him. 'You mean—it was your father who knew my grandfather!'

'That's right. Unfortunately, my father retired eight years ago through ill health. I am now the chairman of Kyle Textiles. My name is Jarrod Kyle, too.'

'Oh, I see!' Sara's expression cleared. 'That explains it.'

'Yes, to you perhaps,' remarked Jarrod thoughtfully, his eyes appraising her very thoroughly, so that Sara felt uncomfortable under his scrutiny. This was definitely a situation her grandfather had not envisaged when he added that awful clause to the will. 'Tell me,' went on Jarrod, 'do you have any relations at all?'

Sara flushed. 'No,' she replied, nervously brushing back the swathe of heavy chestnut hair that swung silkily to her shoulders.

'And what would you have done had that particular clause not been added to your grandfather's will?'

Her flush deepened. She had the feeling he was being slightly sardonic, even though his expression had not changed. 'I—I suppose I should have left school immediately and got a job,' she said defensively.

'As what?'

She shrugged awkwardly. 'I don't know—in an office, or perhaps as a trainee nurse! The nursing profession always appealed to me.'

'Hmn!' He seemed to grow tired of this questioning, and turned away, walking to the window overlooking the sparse patch of lawn in front of the small house. 'Nevertheless, the clause was added, so'—he swung round again—'collect your coat. We're leaving!'

'Leaving?' Sara's greenish-hazel eyes were wide. *'Leaving?'*

'Only temporarily, for the moment,' he replied smoothly. 'My father wants to meet you. Afterwards —well, afterwards we shall see!' he finished enigmatically.

Sara wanted to argue with him. She wanted to say she knew nothing about him and that she didn't want to leave all that was known and familiar to her for some unknown destination, but her position was too nebulous, too helpless, for her to be intrepid enough to argue with the chairman of Kyle Textiles. He might not be as old as her grandfather, but he was obviously in his thirties, or thereabouts, and that seemed a great age to someone who was only seventeen. So she gave him a reluctant nod and went to explain the position to Mrs. Mason.

The white Mercedes was superbly comfortable, and even after Jarrod had left Bridchester and was moving swiftly along the road towards Malthorpe in the Forest she felt little sensation of speed. In fact she was a little bemused by the whole operation, and couldn't help but see it in the light of a crazy dream that could not be substantiated with fact.

Jarrod Kyle was wearing a dark lounge suit, a thick fur-collared overcoat overall, and even with her limited experience of life and material possessions, she could tell his clothes were expensively tailored. Her own fur-collared blue tweed, which she had donned in preference to her dark school duffle coat, looked cheap and inelegant by comparison, and she felt faint stirrings of alarm when she contemplated meeting Jarrod Kyle senior. His son was intimidating enough for both of them. He did not seem particularly pleased about something, she thought, and as she had little to go on she could only assume it had something to do with her.

She sighed, and he glanced her way. 'Tell me,' he said, 'have you spent any time away from Bridchester?'

Sara frowned thoughtfully. 'Only on holidays,' she answered. 'I've been to Blackpool twice, and to London, and once we went to Hastings.'

'I see. You've never been abroad, I gather.'

'No, I'm afraid not.' She looked across at him solemnly. 'I—I suppose you have.'

'Some,' he replied non-committally, and Sara realised it had been a stupid, childish question to a man like him. 'What are your interests, then?' he was asking now. 'What do you do when you're not at school?'

She frowned. 'Well—I like reading, of course, and records, and occasionally Grandfather used to take me to the theatre in Leeds, or even a cinema.'

'What is your favourite subject at school?'

'Do you mean my favourite subject—or the one I'm best at?' she asked candidly.

He looked half-amused. 'Is there a difference?'

'Yes. My favourite subject is English Lit., but I'm best at art.'

'Art!' Jarrod sounded surprised. 'And don't you like art?'

'Well, I passed in "O" level, and I quite like messing about, but Miss Finch, our art teacher, is a bit of a—well——' She was obviously stumped for a suitable word. 'Anyway, nobody likes her, so I suppose that's why I'm not keen on art,' she finished, sighing.

Jarrod swung the car off the main road on to a minor road which led to Malthorpe in the Forest. As the wheel slid expertly through his hands, Sara noticed the length of his fingers. Long and tanned, they looked hard, capable hands, a broad gold signet ring inset with a huge ruby on the little finger of the right.

It was quite dark when they halted at the lodge gates and Jarrod sounded the horn which brought Hedley to the gate. Sara looked at him again and trembled a little.

Jarrod, as though aware of her nervousness, said:

'Don't be alarmed. This is routine procedure. My father has a valuable collection of antiques which he wants to protect.'

'I see.' Sara bit her lip. Even in the gloom the place had an air of grandeur to which she was not accustomed, and the thought of the interview ahead filled her with trepidation.

The car halted before the front doors which opened as if by magic. 'That is our butler, Morris,' murmured Jarrod, rather mockingly, glancing her way. 'I'm convinced he has installed radar in the kitchen quarters so that he knows when any car is within a certain radius.'

Sara couldn't prevent the smile that lifted the corners of her mouth. Although Jarrod had said nothing to reassure her, his manner was more relaxed, probably because he's got me off his hands, she thought uncharitably, and he seemed to be trying to relax her also. As Jarrod slid out, she got out too without waiting for anyone's assistance, and stood looking awkwardly at the tall, imposing figure of Alister Morris.

'Good evening, Mr. Jarrod,' he was saying smoothly. 'Your father is waiting for you in the lounge.'

'Thank you, Morris.' Jarrod mounted the steps easily, and then looked back at Sara standing lost and alone at the foot of the steps. 'Come on, Sara Robins. Surely you're not afraid!' His tone was mocking.

Sara stiffened and climbed the steps too. 'No, Mr. Kyle, I'm not afraid,' she said tautly, and he smiled sardonically.

'Are you not? Then you must indeed be unique.

25

I would have thought these circumstances might represent quite an ordeal to a child like yourself.'

Sara followed Jarrod inside the entrance on to the luxurious blue carpeting of the wide hall. She looked about her in wonder for a moment, and then turned her attention to Jarrod, who was watching her with undisguised sarcasm.

'My grandfather used to say that only a fool was afraid,' she said in small clear voice. 'A coward dies as swiftly as a brave man.'

Jarrod bowed his head in mocking salute to her comments. 'I think your grandfather had quite a lot to commend him,' he said. 'After all, it's not every man who thinks to endow his granddaughter with the richest guardian available!'

Sara stared at him in shocked surprise. 'What do you mean by that, Mr. Kyle?' she exclaimed.

'My son is a cynic, Sara,' said a voice from behind her. 'I heard you arrive, my dear. Welcome to Malthorpe Hall.'

CHAPTER TWO

SARA swung round to confront an older edition of Jarrod Kyle. His father had grey hair, of course, and was a little stooped, but otherwise they were very alike, only the deeply carved lines on the older man's face belying his age. He was smiling warmly, and looked unlike the formidable individual she had conjured up in her imagination.

'You're—Mr. Kyle?' she said awkwardly. 'The Mr. Kyle who knew my grandfather?'

'Correct on both points.' J.K. looked across at the butler. 'Close the door, Morris, and take Miss Robins' coat. Come along, my dear. I'm having tea served in the lounge.' He gave his son a questioning glance. 'Will you join us, Jarrod?'

Jarrod Kyle was removing his own overcoat with lazy movements, and Sara became aware of a strange quickening of her senses. She couldn't understand it, certainly she had never felt anything like it before, but there was something about Jarrod Kyle that disturbed her. Obviously, she had never met a man like him before, but it wasn't only that. Mentally, she shook herself. She was being fanciful, because of the strangeness of her surroundings.

He shook his head now in reply to his father's question. 'No, I don't think so, J.K. You have your afternoon tea. I need something a little stronger.'

His father's lips tightened and he turned away. Then he looked back. 'Lauren rang this afternoon,' he remarked casually. 'She wants you to ring her.'

'Does she?' Jarrod was lighting a cigar. 'And what did you tell her?'

His father smiled. 'I told her—you'd been—busy!' His tone was mocking, and Sara was aware of the antagonism between them like a tangible thing in the air.

Jarrod turned to the stairs, taking them two at a time without replying, and his father gave a satisfied little chuckle before taking Sara's arm to lead her into the long, high-ceilinged lounge.

Sara's attention was taken by the magnificent décor. The carpet, cream and thick-piled, was the background for deep red and black chairs and the dark polished wood of a corner cocktail bar. There was an enormous television set combined with a radiogram, while concealed lighting above the high coving drew attention to the extravagantly carved ceiling. It was like something out of a film set, and she gasped.

'Do you like it?' asked J.K., looking pleased.

'I—I think it's marvellous, Mr. Kyle,' she exclaimed. 'I—I didn't know places like this existed in Yorkshire!'

He laughed. 'Oh, Sara, what a refreshingly youthful remark! And you must call me J.K. Everyone does. It at least distinguishes me from my son.'

Sara did not know how to answer, so she merely smiled, and J.K. rang the bell to summon the maid. 'Sit down, Sara,' he said, nodding to a low couch. 'I want to hear all about you—and your grandfather.'

She subsided on to the couch as he indicated, smoothing the skirt of her dark blue pinafore dress. She wondered what the servants would make of her.

She was hardly the usual kind of visitor to Malthorpe Hall. It was so beautifully warm, too, and she thought there would be no need to wear warm clothes in these surroundings.

A neatly uniformed maid brought a tray of tea and placed it on a low table near Sara, and after she had gone, J.K. seated himself opposite her, and said: 'Can you handle a teapot?'

The cups were small and wafer thin, but Sara managed to accomplish the feat of handling the silver teapot without accident, adding cream and sugar to J.K.'s at his instigation, and only cream to her own. There were sandwiches of ham and salmon, and small scones oozing with jam and fresh cream, but she ate very little, her throat still rather constricted with nerves.

J.K. glanced at a gold cigarette box afterwards, and said: 'Did your grandfather allow you to smoke?'

Sara smiled, shaking her head. 'No, not that I was particularly interested—Mr.—I mean J.K.!' She flushed.

'Very good, too. It's a filthy habit in women. But still, it does give one something to do at interviews and suchlike. Anyway, Sara, come on: tell me about yourself. Your school, your plans, what you and old Jeff used to do together.'

He was very easy to talk to, much less frightening than his son, and Sara soon found her nervousness dispersing in the warmth of his interest. She told him about everything, even the Masons, describing her life with such attention to detail that J.K. became really intrigued, to the extent that he forgot the passage of time, and it was only when Morris knocked and entered, interrupting them, that he glanced at his watch.

'Will the young lady be staying for dinner, sir?' Morris asked politely.

'Well, as it's already almost seven o'clock, I think that would be the most sensible course,' said J.K., nodding across at Sara. 'Don't you agree?'

'Oh, but—I mean, I'm not dressed for—dinner,' stammered Sara awkwardly, recalling Jarrod Kyle's presence with some misgivings.

J.K. gave a deprecatory gesture. 'That's of no importance, my dear. I shan't be changing now, and I don't suppose Jarrod is still at home. Eh, Morris?'

'Mr. Jarrod left half an hour ago,' said Morris evenly. 'He told me to tell you he might be late.'

J.K. smiled sardonically. 'Did he? How thoughtful of him! All right, Morris. Dinner for two.'

'Yes, sir.' Morris withdrew, and J.K. rose to his feet and crossed to the cocktail bar.

'What will you have to drink?' he asked. 'You must have something. Something innocuous, of course.'

Sara swallowed hard. 'Wh—what do you suggest?'

'Oh, I don't know—how about a small sherry?'

'Yes. That would be fine.' She relaxed against the red upholstery, thinking with relief that Jarrod would not present his disturbing presence at dinner. Then she frowned. If Jarrod had left, how was she going to get home? 'Mr.—J.K.?'

He glanced round. 'Yes?'

'If—if your son has left—how will I get home? I mean—is there a bus service, or something?'

J.K. shook his head. 'Naturally Potter will take you in the car.'

'Potter?'

'My chauffeur. Now, there you are. I think you'll find that to your liking."

Sara sipped the sherry pensively, wondering where Jarrod Kyle had gone. Obviously he would have plenty of friends and acquaintances in the district. She wondered if he was married. And where was J.K.'s wife?

'Is your wife——?' She halted abruptly. It was none of her business after all. Turning red, she hoped he had not noticed her words. But of course he had, and he said:

'Go on! What were you going to ask? I think you're entitled to ask a few questions yourself. I've done most of the questioning so far. Don't be nervous!'

'Well, I was just going to ask where your wife was,' said Sara.

J.K. nodded. 'My wife is in Jamaica,' he said easily. 'She lives there.'

'Oh!' Sara's mouth belied her astonishment.

He smiled, swallowing some of the Martini in his glass. 'Do you think that is an unconventional relationship? Don't be afraid to say.'

Sara shrugged. 'Well, do you live here?'

'Most of the time,' he nodded.

'Then yes, I do think it's unconventional. Are you divorced?'

'No. Just separated, through choice. Helen is not like me; she likes the social life. She also likes a warm climate. Several years ago she developed a mild congestion of the lungs. She was advised not to winter in England, so'—he shrugged—'she moved to Jamaica'

'And you?'

'Well, for a while—in fact for many years—we had discovered we had nothing in common. Our lives were quite separate. It was a natural course of events that she should eventually leave.'

'How awful!' Sara sighed. 'I am sorry.'

'Why be sorry? Helen is happy, and so am I. We're not enemies. We've been quite civilised about it since Jarrod was about—oh, seven or eight years old.' He poured himself another Martini. 'Helen came from a wealthy Yorkshire family. I think she fell in love with me, although I'm not certain of that. At any rate she was sufficiently interested to marry me, and in so doing provide me with the necessary funds to expand my business.'

Sara's eyes were wide. 'You mean—you married her for her money!'

J.K. lifted his shoulders. 'How cold and calculating you make that sound, Sara. How capable young people are of exposing life to the cold light of day! I would say we married out of a mutual need, at that time. I've repaid Helen every penny of the money she loaned me. I don't consider my actions so despicable.' He sighed, as he watched the revealing expressions crossing her face. 'I suppose you do.'

Sara bit her lip. 'Oh, really—J.K.—it's nothing to do with me. I mean—I don't know all the facts or anything. I'm not your judge.'

'No, perhaps not. But you make me see myself as others might see me.' He gave a chuckle. 'How Jarrod would have enjoyed hearing you bare the basic facts of life! I think sometimes he can be a little cruel himself.'

Remembering Jarrod's mocking, meaningful words in the hall of Malthorpe, Sara thought that was entirely likely.

The evening passed so quickly that Sara could hardly believe it when J.K. told her it was time she was going home. She felt a sense of regret that it should be over so swiftly, but was surprised when J.K. said:

'Will you come again on Thursday? I can't invite you tomorow. Jarrod is entertaining some chaps from the Ministry, and it would all be incredibly boring, anyway.'

Sara slid her arms into her coat. 'Well, yes—I can, if you want me to,' she said a little breathlessly.

J.K. nodded. 'Good, good! I'll look forward to that. Goodnight, Sara.'

'Goodnight, J.K.,' she answered him, and followed Morris out to the chauffeur-driven Rolls that waited at the foot of the steps.

Mrs. Mason was very curious about what had happened when Sara returned to their house in Mead Road. 'What's going to happen to you?' she asked. 'Are you going to live with this Mr. Kyle and his wife?'

Sara sought about awkwardly for words to say. She knew Mrs. Mason of old, and everything she said to her would be spread around the small town of Bridchester within a few days. 'Nothing has been decided yet, Mrs. Mason,' she replied honestly. 'I— I had dinner with the older Mr. Kyle, the one Grandfather used to know. The man who came here —was his son.'

'I see.' Mrs. Mason frowned. 'Did you tell him

you couldn't go on staying here?'

'I don't think we discussed that at all, Mrs. Mason.'

'You didn't? Well, what did you discuss then?'

'Oh, mostly about—Grandfather,' replied Sara, wishing this catechism was over. She ought to have thought about this coming home in the car, and prepared her answers accordingly. 'Do you mind if I go to bed now?'

Mrs. Mason shrugged. 'I suppose so. When will you know what's going on?'

'I'm having dinner with Mr. Kyle again on Thursday evening,' said Sara. 'I—I might have made some plans by then.'

'What sort of plans?'

Sara gave her a desperate look. 'I don't really know. Honestly, Mrs. Mason, I haven't seemed able to make any plans yet. It's been so—so sudden. But I will. I thought of going to see the Matron at the hospital to see if she would take me on as a probationer.'

Mrs. Mason frowned. 'Did you now? Well, our Lily tried that, but she didn't like it.'

Sara could have said that 'their Lily', who was eighteen, didn't like anything that remotely resembled work, but she held her tongue and merely went upstairs to get washed, thus ending the conversation.

On Thursday afternoon, Potter arrived in the Rolls to take her out to Malthorpe Hall, and Mrs. Mason, who had remained silent during the last couple of days, now said, rather spitefully:

'I suppose you'll be thinking you're too good for the likes of us soon, Miss Robins,' as Sara left the house.

Sara stared at her in astonishment. 'Why should I think that, Mrs. Mason?' she asked in surprise.

Mrs. Mason seemed to regret her impulsive tongue. 'Oh, nothing, nothing. Go along with you. And don't be late.'

In the back of the Rolls, Sara felt rather lost and alone. Even the prospect of dinner at Malthorpe Hall did little to assuage her depression. She seemed now to be a representative of neither walks of life. Ostracised and sneered at by Mrs. Mason and her cronies, and tolerated by a man who had once known her grandfather rather well, but who had now passed out of their sphere.

The drive gates were opened at their arrival, and the car sped up the drive to halt at the main entrance. Potter had not spoken on the journey. He had kept the glass partition between the two compartments firmly closed and Sara had not had the heart to attempt any kind of conversation. Besides, he was probably not accustomed to talking with his passengers. They most likely had plenty of other things with which to occupy them. Unlike Sara, who would have been glad of anything to lighten her mood.

She climbed the steps as Morris opened the door, allowing the warm comfortable glow of the lights to illuminate the forecourt. She was ushered inside, and Morris said: 'Good evening, miss. Is it cold out?'

Sara relaxed a little, taking off her coat. 'Yes, it is,' she said quickly. 'I think it's going to snow. The roads are very icy.'

Morris smiled in a friendly way, and then J.K.

came out of a door to the left of the hall. 'Ah, Sara,' he exclaimed, 'you've arrived! Good! Come in here and get warm. Morris, we'll have some tea.'

'Yes, sir.' Morris nodded, and Sara followed J.K. into a room which was lined with books. Another man was sitting by a roaring fire, but he rose to his feet at her entrance, and Sara recognised him as the solicitor who had advised her of the circumstances of her grandfather's will, Mr. Grant.

'Hello, Sara,' he said, smiling encouragingly. 'You look very nice. How are you?'

'Oh, I'm fine, thank you.' Sara looked questioningly at J.K. 'Am I intruding?'

J.K. closed the door. 'Not at all. It's because of you that Joe's here; Mr. Grant, that is. We've been considering ways and means for you, Sara. I knew when we were talking together the other evening that we had a lot in common, or at least, a common sense of humour!' He chuckled. 'At any rate, I liked you, Sara, and I needed time to think, to work things out. Well, I've come to a decision, and if you're agreeable, there's no possible reason why it shouldn't work out.'

Sara was trembling a little, even in the heat of the roaring fire, and she sank down weakly on to a low chair. 'What are you talking about, J.K.?' she asked.

'You—and your future,' replied J.K. 'Look, have you made any plans yet?'

Sara ran her tongue over her lips. 'Well, I rang the Matron at Bridchester General Hospital yesterday, and I've made an appointment to see her later this week. I hoped she'd be able to take me on, as a probationer.'

'I see,' J.K. frowned. 'Is that what you want to do?'

Sara flushed. 'Well, I've always been interested in nursing,' she replied defensively.

'And if your grandfather had been alive? What would you have done then?'

'I expect I should have stayed on at school for another year and taken my "A" levels,' she answered, sighing.

'Hmn. But now, honestly, Sara, if you had a choice, to do anything you wanted to do, what would it be?'

Sara studied her fingers. 'Oh, so many things,' she said, a little unsteadily. 'I mean—I love English and reading, and I enjoy art immensely. I'd like to travel—and to paint!' She lifted her shoulders helplessly. 'So many things!'

J.K. looked pleased, and glanced rather triumphantly at Joe Grant. 'As I thought,' he said, nodding. 'You're a sensible young woman. Well, Sara,' he paused with pleasurable anticipation, 'if you're agreeable, you can come and live with me—here at Malthorpe, for a year. I say, for a year, because nowadays teenagers know their own minds at eighteen, and I don't want you to feel—how shall I put it?—obliged to me, in any way. I'm doing this because *I* want to, just as much as for your sake!'

'Oh, but——' she began hastily.

'No buts.' J.K. compressed his lips firmly for a moment. 'Just listen, Sara. Whatever you decide to do with your life can wait for a year. During that year you could do whatever you wanted to, be yourself, not some confined schoolgirl with a limited range of interests. You could travel. I go to the States quite frequently, Jarrod was practically educated there, and sometimes I think he's more American than English; then I go to Europe—I could even give you a sort of artistic grand tour, if you'd like that.'

Sara turned to Mr. Grant. 'Oh, please,' she said, 'I can't accept this. I know my grandfather put that clause in the will, but he must have been crazy to do so. J.K. isn't even the chairman now, anyway. His son is. Surely he should have some say in the matter!'

'Jarrod will be consulted, of course,' said J.K. irritably. He did not like to be thwarted, or argued with.

'How thoughtful of you, J.K.!' The sardonic voice brought them all to their feet, facing Jarrod Kyle, who had entered silently, and was standing leaning against the door, looking cold and arrogant. He straightened, thrusting his hands into the pockets of his trousers, and allowing his penetrating blue gaze to rest momentarily on each of them. 'It's good of you to consider my feelings, J.K. Extraordinarily good of you!' The sarcasm was very evident. 'The point you all seem to be missing is that by accepting any part of this will, one automatically accepts all of it.' He allowed this to have effect before continuing: 'In other words, Miss Robins has a meal ticket for life, and there's nothing any of you can do about it.'

'That's terrible!' exclaimed Sara, staring at him.

'Yes, terrible,' said J.K. angrily. 'You're talking arrant nonsense, Jarrod. At the most we are responsible for Sara until she is eighteen. After that, even should she want to, which I for one don't believe, she couldn't make any claims against us!'

'Oh no?' Jarrod gave an exasperated sigh. 'Do you honestly imagine you could get away with—well, refusing to support someone who on your own admission had been supported by you for the last year? My God, J.K.! There are times when I think you've reached your dotage. What's happened to that cold business brain you always used to pride yourself on possessing?'

'Obviously I've passed it on to you to add to the one you already had!' exclaimed J.K. furiously. 'How dare you stand there abusing a visitor in your house!'

'Abusing!' Jarrod gave a short laugh. *'Abusing!'* He shook his head. 'I haven't abused anyone. I'm merely stating the facts as I see them. Unlike you, my vision is not clouded by emotion!'

Sara was shaking visibly now. She had never before been a party to such suppressed violence as Jarrod Kyle was displaying. 'Please,' she said. 'Please, don't say any more, any of you! I—I don't want to hear it! I'm sorry—I'm sorry!'

She brushed past Jarrod and jerked open the library door, rushing out into the hall, not knowing where she was going, only wanting to escape. Morris was bringing the tray of tea and halted in surprise.

'Why, Miss Robins, where are you going?'

'Will—will you get my coat, please?' asked Sara, glancing about desperately. 'I'm—I'm going home.'

'Don't bother, Morris,' said J.K.'s voice behind her. 'Sara, Sara, what can I say? You must not allow my son to intimidate you. He—well, he has to be hard in business. It's the only way, and like me, he's

39

used to getting what he wants. You mustn't let our little differences of opinion upset you.'

'*Little differences of opinion*,' echoed Sara wildly. 'You can't call that argument a little difference of opinion! He—he doesn't want me here! He's made that perfectly plain, and for some reason he doesn't trust me either. I—I couldn't be happy—under those circumstances!'

'Oh, Sara!' J.K. sighed heavily. '*I* want you here. Isn't that enough?'

'But you're not my guardian,' she cried. '*He* is!'

'Yes, and as such he ought to be ashamed of himself,' muttered J.K. angrily.

Sara shook her head. 'I want to go home—I mean —back to the Masons, anyway!'

'You see—you have no home!' J.K. caught her arm. 'Sara, be sensible! Jarrod is not here a lot. He spends most of his time in London, or abroad. We won't have to worry about him, I assure you.'

Sara continued to shake her head. 'Please get my coat,' she said tautly. 'I want to leave!'

J.K. compressed his lips, and then summoned Morris. As she put on her coat, he said: 'Won't you change your mind, Sara?'

She moved to the door. 'Thank you for everything, Mr. Kyle—oh, J.K. then,' as he began to protest. 'Is there someone who could take me home?'

'Morris will have advised Potter,' said J.K. wearily. 'I wish you wouldn't do this, Sara.'

Sara managed a faint smile, and then opened the front door and hurried down the steps to the waiting Rolls. She glanced back once at J.K. standing alone at the top of the steps, and felt tears pricking her eyes. He looked alone, too, and she realised that he, too, was lonely. Oh well, she thought sadly, it's too late now. Much too late!

At the beginning of the following week, Sara had her interview with the Matron of the hospital. She was kind and sympathetic, and told her she would know the result of the interview within a few days. After that, it was just a question of waiting, and this Sara did with some impatience. In her free time, too many thoughts came to cloud her mind, and she was longing for a real job of work to banish all thoughts of J.K. and Malthorpe Hall, and most of all Jarrod Kyle, from her brain.

One morning, towards the end of that week, the headmaster of the school came to see her while she was in the school library.

'Ah, there you are Sara,' he said. 'You have a visitor.' He smiled encouragingly. 'He's waiting in my office.'

'A visitor!' exclaimed Sara. 'But—who, sir?'

'A Mr. Kyle,' said the headmaster thoughtfully. 'Kyle. The name's familiar. Of course, Kyle Textiles. Do you know him? Is he some relation of the textile manufacturers?'

Sara felt the colour drain out of her cheeks. 'Is he —is he young—or old?'

'In his thirties, I'd say.'

'Then—then he's the chairman of the corporation,' said Sara, swallowing hard, feeling slightly sick now. 'Did he—did he say why he wanted to see me?'

'The chairman,' the headmaster was musing to himself reflectively. 'What? Oh no, Sara, he didn't say. But he seems very impatient, so I should hurry along if I were you. He's waiting in my office, I'll go and wait in the staff room.'

'Thank you, sir.' Sara managed a faint smile, and then walked quickly along the corridor towards the headmaster's office. As she neared the office, her footsteps slowed, and she wondered desperately what he could want her for. Reaching the door, she hesitated, and then tapped before entering. Jarrod Kyle was sitting on the edge of the headmaster's desk, smoking a cigar, looking tall and lean and disturbingly male. In dark clothes, his tan complementing the uncanny fairness of his hair, he looked every inch the rich, powerful businessman he was. In deference to her femininity, he stood up at her entrance, while she hovered beside the door nervously.

'Either come in or go out,' he said shortly, and with a grimace she entered and closed the door. 'That's better.' He studied her intently for a moment, noticing her pale cheeks, and the faint shadows round her eyes. 'You don't look at all well.'

Sara straightened her shoulders. 'I'm perfectly all right, Mr. Kyle,' she replied coolly.

'Well, I'll take your word for that, for the moment. Tell me, have you fixed yourself up with a job?'

'I'm—I'm waiting for the results of my interview with the Matron of the Bridchester General,' replied Sara carefully. 'I'm very hopeful.'

'I myself contacted the Matron this morning,' he said, surprisingly. 'You were accepted as a student nurse. I told her you would not be going.'

'You did *what*!' Sara stared at him in horror. 'What do you mean by interfering in my affairs! Of course I shall be going! Oh, I shall have to get in touch with her at once——'

'No, you won't,' he interrupted smoothly. 'Because you will not be needing a job. You're coming to live at Malthorpe—at least for the year which my father stipulated the other night!'

Sara raised her head with a little touch of pride. 'Oh no, Mr. Kyle. Now you're mistaken! I have no intention of coming to live at Malthorpe—not now, or at some future date!'

'But you are,' he responded, with equal firmness. 'Now, don't let's waste any more time. I shall see your headmaster myself, and you can collect your things. You won't be coming back here.'

'Don't try your boardroom tactics on me, Mr. Kyle, because they just won't work!' she exclaimed angrily.

'Boardroom tactics!' he said, half amused at her fervour. 'Boardroom tactics! You haven't the first idea what boardroom tactics may be!'

'Well, maybe not,' she said hotly. 'But you can't *make* me do anything!'

He thrust his hands into the pockets of his thick suede car coat. 'Ah well, Miss Robins, there you are wrong,' he said smoothly. 'You're forgetting! However unpleasant you may find the news, I am your guardian, and as such, I have absolute power over you. Unless, of course, you'd care to take me to court to prove otherwise. But somehow I don't think you will. I could employ such a more satisfactory lawyer than you could!'

Sara couldn't believe her ears. 'But why? Why? Heavens, only a week ago you were suggesting I was trying to—well, you know what you said!'

'I know. My opinion has changed very little. However'—he held up a hand as she would have protested—'however, my father is insistent that you be allowed to come to Malthorpe, and he can be very persuasive.'

Sara's eyes mirrored her disbelief. 'Oh really,' she exclaimed. 'I can't believe the hard, powerful Jarrod Kyle, chairman of Kyle Textiles, and Lord of the Universe, could be persuaded by his *father*!' As soon as the words were spoken she was aghast at her own temerity, but instead of censure she saw a reluctant trace of admiration in his blue eyes.

Then, as suddenly, it was gone, and he said quietly: 'My father has a heart condition; that's why he retired as chairman in the first place. Last Friday he had another mild attack. I'm not prepared to risk his health for my own amusement. If he wants you so desperately, then he shall have you.'

Sara's heart softened ever so slightly. 'Does—does J.K. know you're here?'

Jarrod gave her an exasperated look. 'You must be joking! Of course he knows I'm here! Do you imagine I'm doing this to surprise him! Oh no! I'm well aware of his fallibilities. I'm almost certain his attack was contrived, but I'm not prepared to gamble on anything less than a certainty. Therefore, will you go and collect your things, Miss Robins?'

Sara hesitated. 'And if I refuse?'

'I'm pretty certain your heart is softer than mine,' replied Jarrod, stubbing out his cigar lazily. 'You couldn't take that risk either, could you, Miss Robins?' and Sara knew he was right.

CHAPTER THREE

TODAY Jarrod was driving a dark green sports car, and Sara looked at it with some interest as she climbed inside. 'A Ferrari,' remarked Jarrod dryly, as though in answer to her unspoken question. 'Very expensive! Would you like my father to buy you one?'

Sara tightened her lips, not deigning to reply, although his words were hurtful. She would not enter into a battle of wits with a man much more capable of choosing his weapons than she was. Besides, she was vulnerable; he was not.

The engine roared to powerful life, and he drove out of the school playground with some impatience, watched by a group of boys who had been playing football. Sara glanced back at the school rather regretfully, and Jarrod said bitingly: 'Surely a school can't arouse sentimentality!'

Sara's fingers gripped the strap of the leather satchel on her lap. 'Not to someone like you, perhaps,' she replied quietly.

Mead Road was not busy at this hour of the morning, but Mrs. Mason was standing at her gate, talking to her next door neighbour, Mrs. Isherwood. Sara gave a small sigh when she saw them, and Jarrod said: 'Now what's wrong?' He glanced her way, and then back at the two women by the gate. 'Are you afraid of what they might say?' His tone was mocking.

'Oh, you wouldn't understand!' she cried hotly, as he brought the car to a snarling halt beside the two women.

'Credit me with a little common sense,' he said shortly, and pushed open his door and slid out. Leaving Sara to extricate herself, he walked across to Mrs. Mason, looking arrogant and assured. 'Hello again,' he said smoothly. 'You may be relieved to know that Sara is leaving!'

'Leaving?' Mrs. Mason's voice was shrill, and Sara's heart sank to her shoes. 'Do you mean—she's going to live with you?'

Jarrod smiled lazily. 'With my father, Mrs. Mason. I knew you would be glad to be rid of the responsibility.'

Mrs. Mason was speechless for a moment, and then as Mrs. Isherwood looked at her, daring her to protest, she said: 'Well, I don't know about that, Mr. Kyle.'

'Why?' Jarrod drew out his cigar case and extracted one, lighting it with deliberate slowness. 'You've made it quite plain from the beginning, Mrs. Mason, that you could not keep the child longer than was necessary.'

'I know, but—well, I——'

'You didn't think such a thing would materialise, did you, Mrs. Mason? I really believe you expected Sara to go to the Bridchester General without any further assistance from any of us, isn't that right?'

Mrs. Mason's face was red. 'I didn't think any such thing, and you've no right to say such things,' she replied irritably, as Mrs. Isherwood folded her arms to enjoy this unexpected exchange.

'Well, I'm glad about that,' said Jarrod, glancing

46

round to where Sara was standing nervously beside the car. 'Go and pack your things, Sara. If you need any help——'

Sara shook her head, and approached them, passing Mrs. Mason as she entered the gate. Mrs. Mason looked at her piercingly. 'So you're leaving,' she said tartly.

Sara nodded uncomfortably.

'Hmn!' Mrs. Mason said no more, and for the first time Sara was glad of Jarrod's presence.

It did not take long to pack her things, and when she came out again, carrying her cases, Jarrod was leaning on the bonnet of the car watching Mrs. Mason as she continued her conversation, now somewhat stilted, with Mrs. Isherwood. Straightening, Jarrod threw away the butt of his cigar and came to meet her, taking the cases from her unresisting fingers. Then he looked down at her, his eyes amused. 'That wasn't so bad, was it?' and she shook her head speechlessly.

She thanked Mrs. Mason for her kindness, for she had been kind, even if that kindness had been tinged with bad humour, and then wishing her goodbye she walked to the Ferrari, conscious of the two women's eyes upon her. She could almost feel the other eyes behind lace curtains down the road, all wondering where she was going and who with. Not that they'd have to wait long, she thought drearily, Mrs. Mason would have informed the whole street by the end of the day. No one would be in any doubt as to her position.

Jarrod slid behind the wheel, leaning over to push open the door for her. 'Get in, for God's sake,' he muttered. 'No one's got a shotgun on your back!'

Sara compressed her lips, and did as he said, realising he was perfectly aware of her feelings. Then he turned the ignition and the car roared to life. Sara sank back against the soft leather and sighed.

'Well, it's over,' he remarked, as he turned out of Mead Road into Bridchester High Street. 'What a timid kid you are! Hell, I don't ever remember being like that!'

'I don't suppose you ever were,' Sara flared, her emotions disturbed by his indifference.

He gave a short laugh. 'That's better, Sara. Show a bit of spirit! The life you're going to be leading, you're going to be meeting young men and boys who will positively eat you if you continue to act like a mouse!'

'Men like you?' she asked angrily, unthinkingly.

Jarrod's expression was sardonic. 'Hardly, kid! I don't come into either of those categories! But I shall be watching just the same, and I'm expecting a great deal of amusement out of the spectacle!'

'You are a—a—*brute*!' she exclaimed, clenching her fists tightly.

'Oh, am I?' he mocked her. 'Well, you keep on remembering that, and we'll get along fine!'

Sara was given her own room at Malthorpe Hall. When Hester, the maid, showed her into it, she could not suppress the gasp of pure delight that escaped her. Hester, who was in her fifties, looked on benevolently, as Sara swung round examining everything with an engulfing gaze. The carpet, soft and pale pink, flowed into every corner. A long fitted unit of teakwood supplied a double wardrobe and dressing-table, above which a making-up light was fitted. The bed, a large divan, was covered with a nylon fitted quilt, and the curtains of lilac-striped brocade were reflected in the colour of the bed-spread. Hester waited for a moment, and then crossed the room to open a door at the far side.

'This is your bathroom, Miss Sara,' she said, smiling, and Sara walked quickly across to peep into a large mirror-walled room, with a large step-in bath of pink porcelain. The shelf above the pedestal basin was filled with make-up, skin creams, talcum powders and bath oils, and Sara thought she would spend hours experimenting with them. Her only possessions at the moment in the way of cosmetics were a pink lipstick and an eye-liner, which she had only used once. However, as her skin was creamy coloured, and her dark brows and lashes matched the colour of her hair, she did not really need a lot of make-up.

Now she looked at Hester with unconcealed pleasure, and said: 'Thank you, very much.'

Hester smiled dryly, and walked to the door. 'Don't thank me, Miss Sara,' she exclaimed depre-catingly. 'You've Mr. Kyle to thank.'

'Jarrod!' exclaimed Sara, almost without think-ing, and she saw the maid's lips tighten.

'No, not Mr. Jarrod, miss, Mr. Kyle, senior.'

'Oh!' Sara twisted her hands together, behind her back. 'Oh yes, of course.'

'Lunch is in fifteen minutes, miss, if you'll come down to the small lounge.'

'Which is where?'

'If you find your way to the hall, I'm sure some-one will be around to direct you,' replied Hester, and withdrew, closing the door.

After she had gone, Sara flicked open her suitcases, and began to take out her clothes and lay them on the bed. Then she remembered that the maid had said lunch in fifteen minutes, and she hastily took herself off to the bathroom to wash before the meal. It was quite a novelty, having her reflection thrown back at her from every direction, and she spent several minutes turning from side to side, examining her profile from angles she had never seen before. Then, realising time was passing, she hastily washed, cleaned her teeth and ran a comb through her long hair. Her pinafore dress would have to do, she thought, and at least her blouse was clean. Then she left her room, closing the door behind her.

As she walked along the corridor to the head of the flight of stairs, she realised that this was the first time she had been at Malthorpe Hall in daylight, and she was eager to explore outside. Maybe after lunch, she thought, with some excitement. Now that she was actually here, the real meaning of her new circumstances was beginning to catch up with her, and with it came a stomach-churning sense of anticipation. After all, she was only seventeen, and only human, and there were so many things to look forward to. Her steps lightened, and she ran down the stairs, jumping the last two down on to the hall carpet.

Morris was standing in the hall, sorting through some letters on a silver salver. He smiled at her youthful exuberance, and said: 'I gather you found your room satisfactory, miss.'

'Satisfactory!' exclaimed Sara, smiling. 'It's wonderful! Oh, Morris, I'm so excited suddenly, I don't think I could eat a thing!'

Morris chuckled, and Sara thought she was going to like him very much. He was not at all like the butlers of her imagination, who were always elderly, portly gentlemen, with protruberant eyes. Morris was tall, but slim, and only in his late forties, she estimated.

'I'm sure you'll find lunch very exciting,' he remarked now. 'Do you know where Mr. Jarrod and his father are?'

At the mention of Jarrod's name, Sara subsided somewhat. 'No—no, I don't,' she said.

'Then come this way.' He led the way across the hall and through the arched entrance to a room Sara had not seen before. It was slightly smaller than the lounge, but equally luxurious, with a red carpet, and a suite of green brocade. She thought it was very probably a room used by ladies in bygone days for sewing or needlework, but now it was entirely contemporary in design, huge fitted cupboards of finely polished wood, with glass doors, housing some of J.K.'s collection of jade and porcelain.

J.K. himself came to meet her, smiling warmly. 'Well, Sara,' he said. 'Do you think you can be happy here?'

'Oh, J.K., what a question!' Sara enthused, and then saw that a young woman was lounging negligently on the low couch, watching her through narrowed blue eyes. She looked soignée and elegant, with red-gold curls cut short, and framing her head like a halo. Her features were narrow and arresting, and she was very slim. As though becoming aware of the direction of Sara's attention, J.K. turned, drawing Sara forward.

'Come and meet Lauren Maxwell,' he said. 'Lauren, this is Sara, Sara Robins.'

Lauren Maxwell did not rise to her feet, but extended a languid hand which Sara shook awkwardly. Seeing the older woman here made her realise more clearly than anything had yet done what a lot she had to learn if she was to mix with the kind of people J.K. mixed with. Lauren was eyeing her pinafore dress with a mixture of amusement and distaste, and Sara saw that Lauren was wearing jodhpurs and a chunky yellow sweater. Beneath the sweater that was open she could see a lemon heavy silk blouse, and everything about her spelt sophistication.

'So you're Sara,' she was saying. 'I've been—dying to meet you!'

Sara was certain that Lauren Maxwell had absolutely no interest in anyone like herself, except in so far as it affected her life, and as Sara did not know anything about her she could not be sure just who she was. J.K. elucidated with his next words.

'Lauren's family own the land that marches with ours,' he explained. 'Naturally, we've known each other for years, since Lauren was a child, and she treats Malthorpe as her second home.'

Lauren gave J.K. a provocative smile. 'Darling J.K.,' she said.

Sara wondered why Lauren's words caused such a sinking feeling in her stomach. Maybe because when she had thought of living at Malthorpe herself she had not really considered that anyone other than J.K. and Jarrod Kyle would be involved. She didn't know why, but she had the strongest feeling that she wasn't going to like Lauren Maxwell, which was absolutely ridiculous.

J.K. crossed to a tray of drinks on a nearby table, and said: 'What will you drink, Sara? Sherry—or just some cordial?'

'Er—cordial, please,' said Sara, staying near the entrance as though planning her escape, and when J.K. handed her a tall glass of lime and lemon he drew her into the room and insisted that she seated herself. She perched on the edge of an armchair, hoping there were no ladders in her tights, aware that Lauren was scrutinising her very thoroughly, but discreetly, as though not wanting J.K. to notice.

'I wish Jarrod would hurry up,' said Lauren, stretching, and reaching for a cigarette from the box on the coffee table beside her. 'I'm starving!'

J.K. nodded. 'Well, Sheridan has been trying to get in touch with him for the past two days, but as I've been—well, rather under the weather, Jarrod has managed to put him off.'

Lauren grimaced. 'Business!' she said scathingly. 'Why doesn't Jarrod just get himself a man who can take over in his absence and give himself more free time?'

'Because he likes it,' said J.K. not without some satisfaction. 'Kyle Textiles wouldn't be half so successful without Jarrod's personality.' He gave her a wry look.

'You mean—the way he has with women, don't you?' Lauren commented, rather coolly, and J.K. shrugged his shoulders.

'Now what have women to do with the world of high finance?' remarked Jarrod lazily, strolling into the room. 'Lauren, you'll be giving our guest a

53

very bad impression of me, if she hasn't already got one, of course.'

Lauren wriggled in her seat, like a sleepy cat. 'Come and sit down, darling, and I'll demonstrate if you like.'

'That won't be necessary,' he replied, glancing mockingly at Sara. 'Do you think you're going to like it here, Sara Robins?'

Sara shook her head. 'As I've only just arrived, I can't be absolutely certain,' she replied, with some temerity, and he gave her another appraising look.

'Well, I'm quite sure J.K. will endeavour to accommodate you in every way he can!' he murmured, and walking across to the drinks tray he poured himself a large whisky. Then he looked at J.K. 'I'm leaving after lunch,' he said, and swallowed the whisky at a gulp.

'Oh, Jarrod!' Lauren's voice was reproachful. 'Is that necessary?'

'I'm afraid so, *darling*,' Jarrod replied mockingly. 'There's a meeting tomorrow of the stockholders, and as we've speculating over this deal with Mansons, the American synthetics group, I think I ought to attend and show confidence in their backing.'

Lauren made a face at him. 'Honestly, Jarrod, you've only been back from the West Indies two weeks, and already you're involving yourself right up to your chin. Heavens, the place ran on its own while you were away. Surely you could have waited until the beginning of next week to take up the reins? There's the Hunt Ball on Saturday, and you know you promised to take me. After all, this is your home, and you should show some interest in county affairs!'

Jarrod was prevented from replying by the arrival of Morris who announced that lunch was ready. They ate in the morning-room, which opened off this small lounge. Seated round a small circular table, it was quite an intimate meal, and Sara half-wished they had been sitting at more distance from one another, as such close scrutiny made her nervous, and she fumbled her cutlery, and once dropped a spoon on to the carpet. The meal, a melon cocktail followed by mixed grill and strawberry mousse, was delicious, and even her nervousness could not prevent Sara from enjoying it. She was relieved also that Jarrod was leaving for London the same day. It would give her the opportunity to become orientated to her new suroundings before his return.

When lunch was over, and the men and Lauren were having liqueurs with their coffee, J.K. said: 'This afternoon I'll give you a guided tour of inspection, Sara. I think you'll enjoy that.'

'Oh, I will!' Sara's face lit up. 'I've never seen outside at all. Both times I've been here it was dark when I arrived.'

Lauren looked bored. 'My dear child, on a cold, foggy January afternoon, I should have thought a seat by the fire would have been more your milieu!'

Sara's cheeks burned. 'There isn't much fog now, Miss Maxwell,' she said defensively. 'But of course, if J.K. doesn't want to venture out——'

'Nonsense!' exclaimed J.K. 'Of course we'll go out. I want to show you the stables, and Daviot, my man, will teach you to ride in the near future. You can't ride, can you?'

'Well, I've been to riding school with some school

friends a couple of times,' said Sara, 'but I didn't get very expert.'

'Good!' J.K. rubbed his hands together. 'Good. At least you won't be a complete novice.'

Jarrod rose to his feet. 'I can see you are going to have plenty with which to occupy your time, Sara,' he said sardonically. 'As my father seems to have attained his second childhood, you should be good company for one another.'

Lauren laughed a little behind her hand, and then she rose too. J.K. didn't seem at all disturbed. 'You're perhaps jealous, eh, Jarrod? After all, it's time you were married, with children of your own. It's a pity you're so busy all the time. You miss a great deal of enjoyment that way.'

Jarrod shrugged. 'You think Sara would like me as a father-figure?' he asked lazily. 'I'm sure she ought to have some say in that.'

Sara bent her head, wishing they would not argue in front of her. 'I think you delight in mocking me, Mr. Kyle,' she said candidly. 'But so far as seeing you as a father-figure is concerned, I'd rather not see myself playing Trilby to your Svengali!'

J.K. gave a delighted chuckle, and even Jarrod smiled. '*Touché!*' he said, giving her a slight bow, and then he looked down at Lauren. 'What are you going to do now?'

Lauren sighed. 'Ride back to Hazeldene, I suppose,' she replied shortly, rubbing her nose with a slender finger. 'Unless, you've got any other ideas?'

Jarrod shook his head. 'Not right now, Lauren. Look, I've got to get back, but I'll try and make it for the ball on Saturday!'

'You will!' Lauren's eyes were round. 'Oh, darling, I could hug you!'

Jarrod looked cynical. 'Don't bank on it, Lauren. Just leave it open. I'll ring you some time Saturday, and let you know what's going on!'

And with that she had to be content. Jarrod left the room to get ready to leave, and she followed him, wishing J.K. goodbye, and giving Sara a rather taunting departing smile. Sara relaxed after they had gone, and J.K. said:

'What's wrong? Lauren rub you up the wrong way?'

Sara got to her feet restlessly. 'Something like that.'

'Never mind. Jarrod's the attraction here. When he's away we seldom see her, so don't be alarmed. She's all right, so long as you don't let her get the upper hand. If she thinks she can sit on you, she will, but somehow I think she's realised you're not the timid mouse she thought you!'

Jarrod left soon after, roaring away in the green Ferrari. 'He'll kill himself with those cars one of these days,' said J.K. gloomily, as the car disappeared down the drive. Then he forgot his anxiety in the enjoyment of showing Sara his domain.

There was so much to see that Sara almost grew tired of exclaiming at things. The house itself, with its lounges and dining-rooms, studies and library, bedrooms and bathrooms, all exquisitely appointed, and beautifully warm from the powerful central heating system, was the first item on their agenda, and Sara was even allowed into a strong-room that J.K. had had added to the building to house his collection of pictures. Although Sara found some of the pictures pleasant to look at, she couldn't see any point in collecting something and then locking it away out of sight of everyone, but she refrained from offering her opinion. The objects in the glass cases were much more to her liking, although she trembled when she held an almost priceless piece of porcelain in her hands. There was a jade chess set that really charmed her, and J.K. said:

'I don't suppose you play, do you, Sara?'

She smiled. 'As a matter of fact I do. Although not very well,' she continued. 'Grandfather and I used to play every week. He loved chess.'

'Yes, I know. He and I used to play many years ago.' J.K. sighed. 'Very well, then. We shall make one evening of the week our chess evening, right?'

'Right,' she laughed.

Outside he showed her the stables. There were several horses, a powerful hunter called Apollo, two mares, Persephone and Athena, and a white stallion called Alexander. 'Do you like the predominantly Greek sound to their names?' J.K. asked smilingly. 'I chose them. Jarrod and I spent several months in Greece a few years ago, and I became quite obsessed with mythology.'

Sara stroked Athena's nose. 'I adore mythology myself,' she confessed. 'Those marvellous stories of Homer!'

J.K. seemed pleased. 'It's like I said, Sara. We've got plenty in common. In the spring we'll go to Hellenus, and you can see the islands for yourself.'

'Hellenus?'

'It's an island in the Aegean. I have a villa there. We can spend some time cruising in the area if you'd like to.'

'Oh, J.K.!' Sara shook her head. 'Are you sure? I mean—my being here. We've never discussed it to-day.'

'What's to discuss? I wanted you here, and truth-fully, you wanted to come.'

'Yes,' Sara nodded, thrusting her hands into the pockets of her coat. 'Yes, I wanted to come, but not for the reasons Jarrod imagines.'

'To hell with Jarrod and his reasons. He has a mercenary mind. Besides, he's got so used to fight-ing his way around the concrete jungle of big business that he's forgotten there are honest, decent people left in the world.'

Sara shrugged her slim shoulders. She didn't want to discuss Jarrod Kyle. She didn't want to bring his disturbing presence back, and yet deep inside her she had an awareness of him, a kind of warning system that told her it would not be so simple to shed all thoughts of him. There was something about him, something that aroused her anger and her sensual system all at once. It was a sensation she had never before experienced. Certainly, she told herself with some vehemence, it was not a sexual thing. She was not without some knowledge of men. Her grandfather had seen that she was fully aware of the dangers of promiscuity from a very early age, and at seventeen she had had several youthful en-counters, dates with boys, and the usual kind of gentle embraces most girls of her age had experi-enced. Jarrod Kyle was entirely different from that. Her grandfather had told that love was a warm, gentle emotion that one knew immediately was dif-ferent from casual encounters. The hot, passionate violence displayed on the television screen when men and women made love was not of a lasting variety, and should be avoided at all costs. Too much kissing and petting was dangerous, and a girl should keep herself pure for her husband. All this her grandfather had told her. What he hadn't mentioned was the hot flush that seemed to spread all over her body when Jarrod Kyle made fun of her; the awareness of her own vulnerability in his presence; and most of all the knowledge that he could terrify and excite her all at once, making her totally aware of him.

J.K. was watching her with narrowed eyes. 'Now what are you thinking?' he asked.

Sara flushed, shaking her head. 'Nothing of importance, J.K.'

Later, back in the lounge having afternoon tea, J.K. said: 'Tomorrow we will drive into Leeds. I have a mind to see you in some decent modern young clothes.'

Sara stared at him. 'Oh, but I have other clothes,' she exclaimed. 'But before lunch I was so distracted by the mirrors in the bathroom that I didn't give myself time to change.'

J.K. shook his head. 'No, Sara, that won't do, my dear. Now, let me tell you something, without you taking offence. Your clothes are nice, and obviously the best your grandfather could afford.' He coughed a little. 'But you must understand, Sara, no matter how uncomfortable my words may sound, you're going to be meeting people with a great deal of money and influence, who will expect you—as Jarrod's ward—to be suitably attired. By suitably attired, I mean in clothes fitting to your position.'

Sara swallowed. 'But—but I have no real position!' she said

'On the contrary,' J.K. sounded annoyed, 'of course you have a position. Regardless of what Jarrod may say or do, you are to be treated here as the daughter I never had. My dear, I always wanted a daughter, but in the beginning Helen couldn't, and then later—she wouldn't! What could I do?'

'You could have adopted a child,' said Sara thoughtfully.

'I know, I know. But that wouldn't have been the same. My dear, you may not believe this, but I was very fond of Jeff Robins. He and I didn't see anything of one another in latter years, but I didn't stop remembering him, and obviously he still remembered me."

'In this way,' said Sara dryly. 'He unloaded his granddaughter on to you!'

'Oh, don't be bitter!' J.K. sounded angry now. 'Sara, for heaven's sake, I believe you're allowing Jarrod's attitude to play some part in this. I have taken Jarrod's place, if not in law then in fact, and there's nothing he can—or wants to—do about it!' He sighed. 'Give him the credit for a little decency, Sara. There are thousands, no, millions of people who depend on him for their livelihood. If, in the course of his job, he has become hard, then that's how he should be. You couldn't have a man in Jarrod's position who went around listening to every sob-story thrown his way. Yours was an exceptional case, but only to me! To Jarrod, you were just another unwanted responsibility.'

'I suppose so,' murmured Sara, pouring J.K. a second cup of tea, and helping herself to a hot scone.

'Can I ask a question now?'

'Of course. You're entitled to ask anything you like.'

'Then—what is Jarrod's relationship with Miss Maxwell?'

'Lauren?' J.K. smiled. 'I thought that might intrigue you. Lauren has known Jarrod for years, as I told you. She's younger than he is, of course, but there's never been anyone else for her since she met him.'

'I see. And Jarrod?'

J.K. lay back in his chair. 'Jarrod! Hmn! That's quite a question you've asked there, Sara. Jarrod is quite an unknown quantity, even to me.' He frowned thoughtfully. 'In London there's a girl called Tracy Merrick. Her father is a doctor in Harley Street, a psychiatrist, actually. She's a fashion model, free-lance; seems to have plenty of free time, if you ask me. Anyway, she goes everywhere with Jarrod when he's in town. She's been here a couple of times, and she and Lauren eye one another up like cats before battle commences! Jarrod seems to like both of them, certainly they both want him, but I honestly don't think he's ready to make a choice yet. He's thirty-five this year. He ought to be thinking seriously of marrying and having a family, but he likes his freedom too much. He was in Jamaica for six weeks over Christmas and New Year, staying with Helen—his mother, you know, and if he'd been keen on either one of them you would have thought he would have taken one with him. But he went alone, and Lauren went to Switzerland with her parents instead.'

'I see.' Sara bent her head. 'And which do you

62

prefer?'

J.K. put his cup back into his saucer. 'Well, naturally I know most about Lauren, so you could say I'd prefer her, but I don't know which of them will make him happy. Tonight, for example, he'll arrive back at his apartment—you must go there some time, by the way, it's really something, and he'll change and ring Tracy, and take her out to some blasted nightclub, and be out till all the God-awful hours of the morning, and then take a couple of hours' sleep before attending that meeting of the shareholders, in the morning. Some life he leads!'

Sara couldn't suppress a small smile. 'You sound jealous,' she remarked dryly.

J.K. laughed. 'Dammit, I am!' he said cheerfully.

CHAPTER FOUR

On Friday, they did as J.K. had suggested and drove into Leeds. There was an exclusive ladies' dress shop there called 'Martelle' and it was here that J.K. told the chauffeur to take them. Small and insignificant outside, inside was a world that Sara had never even known existed, outside of London perhaps. J.K. knew exactly what he wanted, he had good dress sense, and the teenage styles at present in vogue suited Sara's slim, yet rounded, body to perfection. Her chestnut colouring looked best with vivid colours, bright reds and blues, greens and yellows, and some of the more subtle colours like a dark shade of mustard, and a deep purple. Sara, trying on dresses and slack suits, assumed they would buy two or three outfits, but J.K. had more ambitious plans. He bought everything he liked her wearing, including two slack suits, day dresses and more exciting styles for evening wear, a thick mohair coat with a half belt at the back and a Swedish lamb car coat with slits up the side, pants and blouses, cardigans and sweaters. Sara protested when she saw the ever-increasing pile of parcels, but J.K. was enjoying himself, and she realised that some of what Jarrod had hinted might conceivably be true, so far as J.K. was concerned. She was a novelty to him, but sometimes they wore off, she thought with some misgivings.

Later they visited a shoe shop and she was supplied with several pairs of shoes and slippers, and a pair of knee-length soft leather boots which hugged her slender legs. By now, Sara had given up protesting, and a little of her enjoyment had gone out of the day.

Then it was home for afternoon tea, and later dinner, just the two of them together. Sara preferred J.K. at home; there he was just a kind, amusing companion, and she could forget the differences in their backgrounds. And yet her background was now the same as his, which troubled her some.

On Saturday morning Jarrod phoned to say he would not be able to make it for the Hunt Ball. J.K. had mentioned the event to Sara, but she had not showed any great interest. She did not feel up to being taken to an event like that, and paraded in front of all the interested eyes of the neighbourhood. She was in the room while J.K. was speaking to Jarrod, and he was annoyed.

'What's stopping you, Jarrod?' he asked bluntly. 'You know damn nicely Lauren is expecting you to take her!'

Jarrod replied, but Sara could not hear his actual words, and J.K. gave an angry exclamation. 'No, not at all. Sara doesn't even want to go!' he bellowed.

Sara felt the trembling sensation beginning inside her that she had noticed a lot lately, and the blood surged to the surface of her skin. So that was why he wasn't coming back: because he thought he might be saddled with her as well as Lauren. She felt furiously angry and upset. How dare he imagine she would expect *him* to escort her!

J.K. slammed the phone down after a few minutes, and then crossed to the drinks tray and poured himself a stiff Scotch. 'Well, to hell with him!' he muttered to himself, and Sara shed her own disturbances, and said:

'What's wrong, J.K.?'

'You must have heard! He's not coming back for the ball. He practically promised Lauren he would!'

'Is he—is he working?'

'No! That's the devil of it! He's going to Monte Carlo for the weekend with Foster Merrick!'

'Foster Merrick?' Sara frowned. 'Who's he?'

'Tracy's father,' muttered J.K., pouring himself a second whisky. 'Oh, no doubt Tracy is going as well, but Foster is only about ten years older than Jarrod and they're good friends.'

'I see.' Sara felt an awful sick tightening of her throat. She ought to have realised that a man like Jarrod Kyle was far more likely to spend his time out of the country than in it, and the kind of entertainment he demanded would be more exciting than a county hunt ball. She supposed he was what her grandfather would have called a member of the 'jet set', and yet at times she had found herself liking him because he made her feel secure. That was a laugh, really! How could a man like that care for security? 'Er—my name was mentioned,' she murmured now. 'What was that about?'

'Huh!' J.K. grunted. 'He suggested I go and take Lauren myself. As if she'd want to go with an old dodderer like me!'

'Oh!' Sara twisted her fingers together in her lap. So much for her imaginings. He obviously didn't even think about her at all, in any connection. She was just a kid his father had taken a fancy to, and

66

who had practically been thrust into their hands. She was the stupid one, even imagining that he might see her as something more than a nuisance!

'Do you want to go, then?' asked J.K., taking her silence for something else.

Sara gasped. 'Me! Heavens, no! I told you, J.K., I'm happier here!'

'All right!' he shrugged. 'Well, I think I'll go and have a bath before dinner. See you later, my dear.'

After he had gone, Sara walked over to the radiogram, opening it and taking out an armful of records. There were plenty of her favourites there like Sammy Davis, Dave Brubeck and Dean Martin, and she thought it would be pleasant just to pick and choose with only herself to please. She put on an L.P. of Dean Martin, fast, beat music that made her swing and sway in time, forgetting for a moment just where she was. She was lost in a world of her own when J.K. returned, and he leaned against the doorpost watching her for a few silent minutes before saying:

'I see you're making yourself at home!'

Sara swung round. 'Oh,' she pressed a hand to her throat. 'You startled me!'

'I'm sorry. Carry on. I like watching you. That dress suits you perfectly.' It was a short-skirted tunic of green wool that drew attention to the curve of her breast and hips, and the length of her legs was not concealed. Her chestnut hair was in disorder about her shoulders, and he said, rather broodingly: 'I didn't realise before, Sara, but do you know you're going to be a beautiful young woman?'

Sara's cheeks burned. 'J.K.!'

'Well, it's true!' he chuckled. 'I think the next

thing I'll buy you will be a car!'

'Oh no! J.K., please. Don't buy me anything else!' Sara sighed. 'It's not that I don't appreciate it, I do, but don't spend any more money!'

'Nonsense. You need a little sports car, a Triumph or a Sprite!'

Sara remembered Jarrod's mocking words about getting his father to buy her a car, and shivered. If he came back and found her with one he would be sure to think the worst.

'J.K.!' she said again, but he merely laughed, and said: 'I'll get in touch with Horners on Monday, and see what they can do for us.'

During the two weeks that followed, Sara became completely used to living at Malthorpe. Her days were filled with activities, and when she wasn't out she spent hours in the library examining the books that J.K. had never even opened. She was learning to ride with Daviot, the stableman, a dour Scot who nevertheless treated her with kindliness and respect, and her own car, a Triumph Spitfire, stood in the garage whenever she was not out with the man from the driving school in Bridchester.

She was gaining poise and confidence quite naturally, and although the only visitors she and J.K. entertained were Lauren Maxwell and her parents, and Doctor Landry from the village, she was gradually learning the art of small talk. Lauren didn't have much to say to her, treating her with a kind of amused tolerance, but her father, Donald Maxwell, was a charming man, and spent time talking with Sara and finding out her interests. Jennifer Maxwell, Lauren's mother, was less friendly.

68

Whether she didn't like the idea of another woman living at Malthorpe, Sara couldn't understand, but certainly she seemed to think Sara had been incredibly lucky to have been accepted there.

And so I have, thought Sara, with some diffidence. It's hardly credible really that I could be so lucky!

One afternoon she told J.K. she was going shopping, but she left the car in Bridchester marketplace, told Potter she would see him there in an hour, and then strolled along the High Street to Mead Road. It was strange, even after only two weeks, everything looked gaunt and unfamiliar, and as it was a wet day, her feet were soon damp in her low-heeled pumps. Reaching Mrs. Mason's house, she knocked at the door, and a few minutes later Lily Mason opened it.

'My God!' she exclaimed rudely, 'it's her ladyship come back, Mum!'

Sara took no notice, and brushed past her down the hall, to where Mrs. Mason was washing up in the kitchen. 'Hello, Mrs. Mason,' she said. 'How are you?'

Mrs. Mason eyed her up and down thoroughly, taking in every detail of the heavy mohair coat and fur cap, and the dripping umbrella in her hand. 'Well, well,' she said. 'So you came back. I never thought you would!'

'Why?'

Mrs Mason sniffed. 'You came to collect your belongings like a blinking rabbit!' she exclaimed. 'Bringing that man with you! Treating me like a stranger in my own home!'

'He didn't even come in!' exclaimed Sara.

'No, but he stood at the gate watching me like a hawk. I didn't dare go into my own house. Not while you were in here.'

'Oh, Mrs. Mason!'

'Don't you *oh, Mrs. Mason* me! Such things aren't for the likes of me!'

'What things?' Sara's eyes were hurt and disturbed.

'You going off with a man like that! Not telling me about it beforehand, or nothing!'

'But I didn't know beforehand. His father had had a heart attack——'

'And was asking for you!' interrupted Mrs. Mason. 'Heck, you don't expect me to believe that one, do you?'

'I don't know what you do mean, quite honestly!' said Sara. 'You know the terms of my grandfather's will as well as anyone!'

'And that man—that Mr. Kyle—is he your guardian, or isn't he?'

'Well, yes——'

'There you are, then!'

'No, you don't understand. I'm not living with Jarrod——'

'So it's Jarrod now, is it?' Mrs. Mason looked belligerent. 'Just you get yourself out of here, young lady, before I gets Cyril to come and deal with you. I want no truck with the likes of you!'

'Mrs. Mason!' Sara was horrified. 'There's nothing I have to be ashamed of. I'm living with that man's father—as his ward!'

'I thought you said he had a heart attack!'

'So he did——'

'Oh, go on, Miss Robins! I want to hear no more

about it. And you needn't bother coming round here, showing off your new clothes and boasting about your new friends. I know what's what. I wasn't born yesterday!'

Sara shook her head, then pushing blindly past Lily who was standing in the hall listening, she ran out of the house. She ran along Mead Road into the High Street, and went straight to the car. Potter was lounging behind the wheel smoking, but he stubbed the cigarette out as soon as he saw Sara, and scrambled out.

'You finished already, miss?' he exclaimed.

Sara slid thankfully into the back of the car. 'Yes, thank you, Potter,' she said, nodding, and shrugging, he slid behind the wheel and set the car in motion. If he could see she was upset, he made no mention of it, and by the time they had reached the outskirts of the town, her tears had dried.

But the hurt remained, and with it the knowledge that she had taken an irrevocable step. She would never have believed even Mrs. Mason could be so horrible. Accusing her of something she must know could never be true. Was that what jealousy was? Had Mrs. Mason allowed her bitterness to overcome her natural inhibitions? Sara didn't know, but as Mrs. Mason had said, she could never go back there again.

Hedley the lodgekeeper waved to her as the car passed through the tall iron gates, and she waved back, putting aside her own problems. For after all, there was nothing she could do to change things now.

Her feet were soaking, and she took her shoes off

as she entered the hall. Morris came to greet her, taking her coat and saying:

'Mr. Kyle is resting. Would you like some tea, Miss Sara?'

'Oh, marvellous!' she said, nodding. 'Could you dry these, please?' She handed him the shoes, and walked across the springy carpet to the lounge, mentally shaking off the sound of Mrs. Mason's coarse voice.

The radiogram stood open, and she smiled to herself as she went over to it. Lying on top was a selection of the current top-twenty records, a surprise J.K. had provided for her, and she put on half a dozen, allowing the loud rhythm of the groups to clear her depression. Turning the volume up, she allowed her own inhibitions to melt away, closing her eyes and dancing with the same abandon she had seen teenagers on television adopt. The noise was quite deafening this close and she did not hear a car arrive, or be conscious of anyone's scrutiny, until she swung round and found Jarrod Kyle leaning against the pillar watching her. Dressed in a thick astrakhan overcoat over a dark blue suit, drops of water sparkling on his slightly ruffled hair, he looked tall and lean and disturbingly attractive, his blue eyes narrowed, long black lashes veiling the expression in their depths.

Sara halted abruptly, conscious of the informality of her attire, her bare feet, and the damp untidy tangle of her hair. She switched off the radiogram, and for a moment the silence seemed as deafening as the music had been. He did not speak, but continued to look at her, his eyes slowly following the length of her body and back to her face again, resting for a heart-shaking moment on her mouth.

Oh God, she thought, feeling her limbs melting under his gaze. Is that how he looked at Lauren, and Tracy? If so it was no wonder they wanted him. She brought herself up short, and turned away abruptly, and as abruptly the spell was broken, and he straightened, and unfastened his overcoat.

Then he turned and walked away, handing his coat to Hester, who had appeared from the direction of the kitchen with Sara's tea tray. He took the tray from Hester, and came back to the lounge, placing it on the low coffee table.

Sara was standing with her back to the radiogram now, hands behind her back, and when he straightened, he said: 'Your tea, Miss Sara,' in a mocking tone.

'Thank you.' With forced nonchalance, she seated herself beside the tray, and said: 'Will you have some, Mr. Kyle?'

He shook his head, lighting himself a cigar. 'I prefer something a little stronger,' he remarked, pouring a whisky from the bottle on the cocktail bar. 'And how are you? I can see that you're quite at home already.' He came to stand in front of her, looking down at her with those intensely blue eyes. She wondered if he was aware of the effect he was having upon her, and decided it was unlikely. After all, *she* was only a silly schoolgirl.

'I'm sorry if the music annoyed you,' she said quietly, lifting her tea cup to her lips.

'Was that what it was?' he remarked mockingly. 'I'd never have guessed!'

Sara wrinkled her nose, but did not argue with him. 'I didn't hear the car,' she said.

'That's hardly surprising, is it?' he murmured sardonically. 'Are you pleased to see me?'

Sara looked up now, startled. 'Should I be?'

Jarrod half-smiled. 'Well, I am your guardian, aren't I?'

'You're many things,' she returned, and bent her head again.

'What is that supposed to mean?' He was interested in spite of himself. 'What has J.K. been telling you?'

'We rarely discuss you,' she retorted. 'And before you find out some other way—I've got a sports car!'

He grinned quite openly now. 'Oh really! What?'

'A Triumph. But I'm just learning to drive at the moment, so you won't see me dashing around the countryside just yet!'

'What a pity! And what a sharp tongue you're getting. A couple of weeks ago' you wouldn't have dared to speak to me like this!'

Sara felt the tell-tale flush rising up her cheeks, much to her annoyance. 'Wouldn't I?' she parried, and he shrugged, and put his cigar between his teeth, unfastening the top button of his shirt, and loosening his tie a little. As usual, his clothes were sleek and expensive, and fitted his lean muscular body closely. She wondered if Lauren Maxwell knew he was home, and if so whether she would be dashing over to spend the evening with him. The idea annoyed her somewhat, and she thought with a sense of dismay that although she saw so little of him, she was becoming absorbed with him intensely.

He flung himself into an easy chair opposite her, and said: 'Has J.K. been buying you clothes, too?'

74

and when she nodded her head, he continued: 'That dress suits you. I like it.'

The dress was honey-coloured crêpe, and clung to her rounded body, leaving a length of shapely leg bare. The neckline was high and cuffed, and had green embroidery on it to match the sleeve cuffs.

Sara studied her fingernails, overwhelmingly conscious of the muscular length of his legs so near her own, and finally looked up to find his eyes closed, the luxuriant length of his lashes resting on his cheeks. She got silently to her feet, intending to go and bathe and tidy her hair, but his eyes opened as she passed his chair, and he said: 'Running away?'

'No. Not at all. Will you excuse me? I want to bathe and change.'

He shrugged. 'I guess so. I'll see you at dinner.'

'You'll be in?' Her eyes widened.

'Shouldn't I be?'

'Will Miss Maxwell be coming?'

'Not unless you've invited her prior to my coming,' he remarked lazily.

'No, of course I haven't.' Sara chewed her lip.

'Good. Put on a pretty dress, and after dinner I'll take you to a party!'

'A party!' Sara's heart thumped.

'Yes, a party. You know—where we all play games and win forfeits!'

'That's not the kind of party you would attend,' she retorted hotly, 'and you know it!'

'No.' He sat up smiling. 'I agree. It's not. But I promise you this party will be as innocuous as that. Right?'

'I don't know. What about J.K.?'

Jarrod got to his feet indolently. 'Sara, you're my

ward, whether you like it or not, and if I say you're coming to a party, you'll come.'

'Will I?' Sara's eyes flashed a little in her flushed face.

His eyes narrowed. 'Well, won't you?'

Sara shivered, then she turned and walked out of the room.

She bathed in the luxurious warmth of the bathroom, filling the bath with scented water, and soaking herself thoroughly. She washed her hair, and dried it with the hair-drier that was also in her bathroom, aware of a rising sense of excitement when she thought of the evening ahead. It was ridiculous to get so disturbed about something like this, she thought, but she couldn't help herself.

Afterwards, she studied the contents of her wardrobe with more interest than she had hitherto shown. All thoughts of Mrs. Mason and that dreadful interview this afternoon were temporarily banished, and she told herself that this was why she was feeling so grateful to Jarrod Kyle.

At last she chose a dress made of rose-coloured chiffon. It had a low round neckline, and long sleeves, and the skirt which fell from a clip just below her breasts was full and floating. It was short and modern, and the style was not particularly girlish. There was nothing she could do with her hair, short of putting it up, and she didn't think she would suit that just yet, so she brushed it till it shone like silk, and fell smoothly to her shoulders. Finally she studied her reflection in the mirror of the wardrobe, pleased with what she saw.

J.K. and Jarrod were both in the small lounge

when she went downstairs, for she could hear their voices. They were discussing the business Jarrod had been working on in London, and Sara wished she did not have to make so obvious an entrance. However, J.K. glimpsed her hovering uncertainly in the hall, and came out to meet her.

'Heavens, child, you look delightful!' he exclaimed in surprise. 'I've never seen you wearing that dress before. It's beautiful!'

Sara smiled uncomfortably, and J.K. drew her into the lounge, where Jarrod, looking serious and enigmatic, awaited them. Tonight, in dark clothes, the fairness of his hair was pronounced, although his skin was so darkly tanned as to be almost swarthy. He handed Sara a tall glass of some pale liquid, which she handled nervously.

'Don't be alarmed,' said J.K. 'It's only Dubonnet with lemonade. Quite a pleasant drink for a young girl like yourself, I should think.' Then he smiled. 'With those clothes, you ought to be going somewhere exciting!'

Sara cast a puzzled look in Jarrod's direction, and he bowed his head sardonically. 'She is going somewhere, J.K.,' he remarked lazily. 'To a party.' He hesitated for a moment. 'With me!'

J.K.'s brows drew together in a frown. 'What do you mean—you're taking her to a party?'

'Exactly what I say,' replied Jarrod, swallowing half his own dry Martini. 'These are very good, J.K. Very dry!'

'Never mind the drinks,' muttered J.K., looking frowningly at Sara. 'What do you mean by suggesting that you should take out this child? She's far too young to go to any of the places you go!'

Jarrod was begining to look bored, Sara thought with a sinking stomach. 'I'm taking her to Howard Lawson's twenty-first birthday party,' he said resignedly. 'You may recall I promised to go several months ago.'

'You promised to take Lauren to the Hunt Ball, but that didn't worry you!' snapped his father.

'No, it didn't,' retorted Jarrod coldly. 'If you must know, I didn't want to take Lauren to the Hunt Ball.'

'So you went to Monte Carlo with Tracy Merrick instead!'

Sara moved uncomfortably. She hated these family quarrels.

'Correction,' Jarrod was saying harshly, 'I went to Monte Carlo with *Foster* Merrick!'

'And Tracy didn't go?'

'No.' Jarrod strode over to the tray of drinks, pouring himself another. 'What do you want to hear, J.K.? Do you want me to describe what I did that night so that Sara will have second thoughts about trusting herself to me, is that it?' He swallowed the drink at a gulp. 'Okay, okay, I went to Monte Carlo with Foster; we went to the Casino, and I gambled—all night! I didn't get drunk—and I didn't sleep with anybody, at least not that night!' He swung round abruptly, banging the glass down on the tray.

Sara felt hot and cold in turns, and J.K. grunted something unintelligible, and said: 'So you're going to Howard's twenty-first, are you?'

Jarrod swung round again. 'If Sara still wants to go!' He looked at Sara questioningly. 'Do you think it's safe, Sara?'

Sara shrugged her slim shoulders. 'Are you quite sure you want to go?'

He gave a mirthless laugh. 'What do you mean by that? That I couldn't possibly enjoy myself at something so tame as a twenty-first party?'

'Sara didn't say that!' growled J.K.

'No, but it was trembling on her tongue.' Jarrod sighed heavily. 'My God, J.K., do you imagine I'm taking Sara to this party to—well, because I'm interested in her now? Sexually, I mean!'

J.K. shrugged. 'No, I guess not!'

'Okay. Now that's the truth! I'm not! So let's hear no more about it! She's my ward, and I'm entitled to spend some time with her, aren't I?'

'Of course.' J.K. was disgruntled. 'All right, Jarrod, I'll shut up. But remember, you'll be driving home!'

'Oh lord!' Jarrod looked incredulous. 'I am fully capable, you know."

'At the moment,' retorted his father.

'At any time,' muttered Jarrod harshly, and strode out of the room.

After he had gone, J.K. looked anxiously at Sara. 'Do you really want to go with him, Sara?' he asked gently.

Sara bent her head. 'Well—I did,' she said awkwardly.

J.K. smote his fist into the palm of his other hand. 'Well, for God's sake, remember who he is, and how old he is! You're an impressionable child, and I don't want you to get hurt.'

Sara sighed now. 'But you heard what he said—he treats me like his kid sister, or even his daughter!'

'I know, I know. Maybe I'm a suspicious old fool,

79

but I know how attractive Jarrod is to women, and I also know that he's only human. If something was offered to him on a plate, he might not be able to refuse!'

'Oh, J.K.!' Now Sara was horrified. 'I'm not like that! Besides, I've no intention of behaving like an idiot. But I am looking forward to going out. It will be a change.'

'Have you been bored here?' asked J.K. anxiously.

Sara smiled. 'No, of course not. It's not that. It's just the excitement of getting ready. Oh, you know how it is!'

'Yes,' said J.K. thoughtfully, and Sara hoped he would not think she was ungrateful.

CHAPTER FIVE

SARA was glad when dinner was over. She didn't eat much even though the Chicken Maryland was delicious, and fresh raspberries in February were a novelty. Jarrod hardly spoke, and when he did it was in answer to something J.K. asked. When the meal was finished, he rose immediately to his feet, and said: 'Well, Sara! Do you still want to come?'

Sara rose too. 'Of course,' she said, looking at J.K. appealingly. 'You don't mind, do you, J.K.?'

He shook his head, and patted her hand when she placed it on his shoulder. Sara left to get her coat. She decided to put on the Swedish lamb, as it was bitterly cold, and the fur was wonderfully warm. It was thigh-length, and practically covered all her dress. A greyish colour, it suited her creamy colouring, and she tucked her hair inside.

Jarrod was waiting for her, the astrakhan coat loose over his lounge suit. He opened the front door, and ushered her outside, closing it behind him. The Ferrari waited at the foot of the steps, and a faint covering of snow warned of the unsettled state of the weather. When they were both in the car, and Jarrod was turning the ignition, Sara said, a trifle breathlessly: 'Is it far?'

Jarrod compressed his lips for a moment. 'A couple of miles,' he replied shortly. 'Have you changed your mind again?'

'No, of course not. I just wondered, that's all.'

Jarrod shrugged, and the car was started smoothly, roaring its way down the drive with expert ease. He was a fast, but expert, driver, and Sara could relax with him even more than with Potter. Once out on to the road, he slowed and said: 'Ice!' by way of explanation. Sara wondered what they would do if it snowed really hard and the roads became blocked. She was wearing her boots and carrying some evening slippers, but even so, it was freezing outside the car, and apart from the coat her clothes were not what her grandfather would have thought suitable for a February night.

The Lawsons' house was outside another village, Melston, and already the drive was lined with cars, and lights and music heralded the party that was in full swing. Jarrod saw her nervous face reflected in the lights from the house as he halted the car, and said: 'Don't worry, honey, you look good enough to eat. All the boys will make a beeline for you!'

Inside, Jarrod was welcomed like a long-lost cousin, and Gina Lawson, Howard's sister, took Sara to the cloakroom. Gina was small and blonde, and about a year older than Sara.

'I say,' she exclaimed, in a friendly way, 'you've found yourself the proverbial fairy godfather, haven't you? Lord, I'd adore to have Jarrod as my guardian!'

Sara smiled, and made some light reply, and then they went out into the hall again to join the rest of the party. Sara was introduced to Mr. and Mrs. Lawson, their teenage son, Hal, and Howard, of course. She was introduced to dozens of people in the course of the next half-hour, but most of the names went out of her head almost as soon as she heard them. The fact that she had come with Jarrod seemed to act as a charm, and no one was anything but delighted to meet her, or so they said. If she caught several of the girls eyeing her a trifle jealously she ignored them, for on the whole they were a friendly group. A buffet supper was served in a long conservatory at the back of the house, while a lounge which stretched from front to back had been cleared for dancing.

After two tomato juices with Mr. and Mrs. Lawson, and Gina, Sara glanced round to see where Jarrod was. They were in the hall between the dancing lounge and the conservatory, and Gina, seeing that Sara was looking about said: 'Come on. We'll go and dance. Jarrod appears to have disappeared.'

In the lounge several couples were dancing to music from a tape recorder, but Jarrod was not there. 'I think he considers himself too old for shindigs of this kind,' confided Gina, smilingly. 'That's why we invited Lauren. She'll look after him.'

'Lauren Maxwell!' Sara sounded slightly shocked, and Gina nodded.

'Yes. You'll know her, too, don't you?'

'Yes, but—oh well.' Sara shut her mouth, and then Howard Lawson came up to them and asked her if she'd dance with him. Deciding she might as well, Sara nodded, and after that, to her surprise, the evening seemed to fly by. Howard had several friends who wanted to dance or talk to her, and she found she had to turn down some dates, even though they insisted they would phone her. Howard seemed the most possessive, and as the night wore on, she danced mainly with him, and sat with him between times.

Then just before midnight, Jarrod appeared, accompanied by Lauren Maxwell. Tonight Lauren looked stunning in a lace trouser suit, slim pants that flared at the ankle, and a brief top that left her midriff bare.

'Hello, darlings,' she exclaimed languidly, her gaze flickering appraisingly over Sara, and dismissing her. 'Have you had a good time?'

Sara looked at Jarrod with candid green eyes. 'You've been a long time,' she said. 'I thought you'd gone home!'

Lauren raised her narrow eyebrows. 'My, my, darling, have you acquired a keeper?'

Jarrod's expression did not change, although his eyes narrowed slightly. 'No, Lauren, Sara merely wanted to let me know she'd noticed my absence!'

Howard put his arm round Sara, almost protectively. 'I've looked after Sara, Jarrod, so it's as well you didn't worry!'

Lauren chuckled. 'Oh well, that's all right then. I say, everybody, it's snowing like hell outside. You're all going to have a terrible drive home. Aren't I lucky, I'm staying the night.'

There were exclamations and dashes to the window to view the white landscape outside, and Jarrod said: 'I think we'd better be going, Sara!'

Howard's grip tightened. 'I'll take Sara home,' he said.

'Don't be an idiot,' said Jarrod impatiently. 'It's a terrible night, as Lauren has just said. I brought Sara, and I'll take her home.'

'Let Sara choose,' said Howard stiffly.

Sara began to protest, when Jarrod caught her wrist, twisting it painfully. 'Get your coat,' he said coolly, daring her to defy him.

Sara wrenched her wrist out of his grasp, intensely aware of the hard coolness of his fingers, and then with a faint apology to Howard she did as she was told.

Goodbyes said to their host and hostess, Sara followed Jarrod down the slippery steps and across the snow covered forecourt to where the Ferrari was waiting. Without waiting for any assistance, she slid inside, and Jarrod brushed the snow off the windscreen, and cleaned the wipers before joining her. He did not speak as he started the vehicle, and Sara waved to Howard standing in the light at the top of the steps. Then they swept down the drive, and out on to the unswept roads outside Melston. It was a filthy night for driving, the snow driving heavily across the windscreen, obscuring most of the view.

Sara sighed, thinking about the weather and the distance between Melston and Malthorpe in the Forest, but Jarrod said tautly:

'What the hell did you mean by asking where I'd been?'

Sara glanced his way, able to see his face in the white light from the banks of snow on either side of them. 'Wasn't I entitled to ask? I thought you said you were taking me to a party? Some party you had!'

'I warn you, Sara——' he muttered, swearing to himself as the car slid across the slippery surface of the road. 'What a blasted night!'

'Well, you must have known what it was like,' remarked Sara dryly. 'Lauren knew the state of the weather. Where were you? In the summer-house, or just her room, as she's staying the night?'

Jarrod ground the car to a halt, and Sara shrank back in her corner, away from the furious expression on his face. 'You bitch!' he muttered angrily. 'My God, J.K. has you well trained!'

Sara shivered. 'I don't know what you mean.'

'Yes, you do, damn you. If you must know, I've been in the Fox and Hounds in Melston, with Lauren. If you don't believe me, get J.K. to ring and enquire. She wanted a drink, and they were all kids at the house, so we *walked* into Melston, right?'

'You don't have to explain yourself to me!' she said, pretending disinterest.

'No, I don't. But I do not intend your nasty little mind to contemplate situations that just did not occur! Even *I* have some pride!'

'Oh, let's just go home!' exclaimed Sara wearily, and Jarrod turned back to the business of driving.

Unfortunately, the car refused to move. The wheels spun helplessly in the slush, and the more he revved the engine, the deeper they sunk. 'God almighty!' he muttered, and Sara felt an unwilling smile creeping to her lips. As though aware of her amusement, he glanced her way, and she put her hand over her mouth guiltily, but he just shook his head. 'We must be crazy,' he muttered, 'conducting a conversation in the middle of a snowstorm, miles from anywhere on a night like this. I'll have to get out and push. Can you drive it?'

Sara hesitated. 'I'm not sure——' she began.

'Hold on, I'll get out. You slide over, and I'll explain. Just don't take off with a rush, and throw me into the slush, will you?'

'I'll try not to,' she said meekly, and he allowed a faint smile to play around his mouth. Then he climbed out, his shoes over their tops in the snow.

But it was no good. The car was deeply embedded, and she couldn't get the gears right. 'Look,' he said, 'do you think you could do the pushing? Oh, I know that sounds rotten, but it only needs the right little push at the right moment, and we'd make it.'

Sara burst out laughing. 'Honestly, what a Galahad you are!' she exclaimed. 'All right, all right. Let me get out.'

So they reversed their positions, and Sara wedged herself against the rear bumper ready to push. Jarrod revved the car, she pushed with all her might, and the car shot away from beneath her, throwing her into the mud and slush and water.

'Oh lord,' she exclaimed, scrambling to her feet, saturated now, and as Jarrod came running back, she said: 'Did you do that on purpose?' rather tearfully.

Jarrod tried not to laugh. 'Oh God, Sara, I'm sorry! Of course I didn't do it on purpose! Come on, let's run to the car.'

'I can't go home like this,' she wailed, 'I'm soaking!'

Jarrod shook his head. 'Well, love, you'll have to. I haven't got anything else you can wear, and if you strip off you'll catch pneumonia. Here——' He stripped off his overcoat, pulling her wet fur off her and putting his warm astrakhan in its place. 'There, is that better?'

'Hmn,' she said, sniffing, and with an exclamation

he lifted her up in his arms and carried her to the Ferrari.

Then, driving as fast as he was able, nearly blinded by the snow, he finished the journey to Malthorpe Hall. J.K. himself was waiting in the hall, and stared in horror at Sara, shivering with cold and shock, wrapped in Jarrod's overcoat.

Behind her Jarrod held up his hand. 'Look,' he said, 'before you start, Sara needs a hot bath, and a warm bed, and you'd better call Doctor Landry just in case.'

'I don't need the doctor,' Sara exclaimed. 'I'm all right,' but her teeth chattered.

'Come on,' said Jarrod impatiently. 'Did you hear what I said, J.K.? Oh, and bring some brandy, too, will you?' Then he swept her off her feet again and made for the stairs.

After that everything got a little blurred. Mary, the upstairs maid, was roused from her bed, and it was she who ran Sara's bath, and helped her into it. Jarrod had deposited her in her bedroom, and left her, and although she saw J.K. several times, and Doctor Landry, she saw no more of Jarrod that night.

In the morning, a cold grey winter's morning, she felt much worse, and when Mary brought her some breakfast on a tray at eight-thirty, Sara was breathing hoarsely, and coughing quite a lot. Despite the brandy and medication she had received the night before, she had caught a chill, and when J.K. arrived in answer to Mary's summons, he immediately recalled Doctor Landry.

Sara couldn't have cared less who they called. She felt hot and cold in turns, and even the hot water bottles wedged on either side of her did little to ease the iciness of her feet and back. She sneezed, and coughed, and took medicines and tablets automatically, wishing she could go to sleep and wake up better.

Once she saw Jarrod beside the bed, but he did not speak to her, and later in the day another man arrived, who examined her thoroughly, before putting her in the charge of a white-clad nurse.

Sleeping and waking alternately, Sara was unaware that her condition almost deteriorated into pneumonia, and only the constant care she received saved her from that. She didn't do much talking, and ate nothing, even though Hester kept bringing trays of light food in the hope that the nurse could persuade her.

Eventually her temperature subsided, and the fever was broken, and then Sara began to feel more like herself. On the morning of the fourth day after her chill, she really felt more normal, and the watery sun penetrating her curtains made her feel good to be alive.

Nurse Macdonald smiled at her cheerfully when she came to see her patient. 'You're feeling much better, aren't you, Miss Robins?' she said, nodding. 'I must let Mr. Kyle know. He's been very worried about you. You gave us all a nasty turn, you know.'

Sara managed a weak smile. 'Which Mr. Kyle do you mean?'

'The older one, of course. He's your guardian, isn't he?'

Sara was about to protest, but then decided it didn't really matter what the nurse thought, and she hadn't the strength to say a lot. She ate a little

89

of the poached egg the nurse brought on a tray, and afterwards, when her face had been washed and her hair combed, Doctor Landry appeared. J.K. was with him, and he sat beside her on the bed, taking her hand.

'Oh, Sara, you've no idea how good it is to see you looking so much better. Nurse tells us you spent a peaceful night, and the fever's gone. Do you know you've been verging on pneumonia for four days? It's been hell, believe me!'

'Has it been so long?' Sara looked surprised. 'I don't remember a lot, just feeling hot and uncomfortable, and having difficulty with my breathing.' She frowned. 'Where—where's Jarrod?'

'He returned to London last night,' replied J.K. shortly. 'There was to be an emergency meeting of the board today. He had to attend.'

'Oh. I thought I hadn't seen much of him,' Sara nodded.

J.K. looked annoyed. 'Nor you have! The idiot! He could have killed you!'

'Killed me?' she echoed. 'Oh no! It wasn't his fault. I was sitting—practically sitting anyway, on the back bumper when the car moved. I just fell in deep water and slush, that was all.'

'Ridiculous! But that still doesn't explain why you had to stop in the first place—getting bedded down in the slush like that!'

'J.K.——' began the doctor warningly, but Sara shook her head.

'It's all right, Doctor, I can explain.'

J.K. ground his teeth together. 'What's to explain? That son of mine will have been fooling around as usual, I suppose!'

'Fooling around? With me?'

J.K. clenched his fists. 'I could kill him!' he muttered.

'Oh, don't be silly,' said Sara tiredly. 'He didn't touch me. He stopped to say something to me, that was all. Heavens, as I recall it, we were arguing, as usual!'

J.K. frowned. 'Is this the truth?'

'Of course. Didn't Jarrod tell you?'

'Almost the same story,' nodded J.K., snorting. 'I didn't believe him. He stayed here, against my better judgement, to assure himself that you were going to be okay, but I wouldn't let him near you!'

'Oh, J.K., I've told you. Jarrod doesn't see me like that!' Sara sighed heavily. 'I wish you wouldn't jump to conclusions. It was all perfectly innocent!'

J.K. had the grace to look a little ashamed, and Doctor Landry said: 'You should go and give him a call. Tell him Sara's on the mend properly now, and apologise for being a mean, suspicious old man!' he smiled.

J.K. got up off the bed, patting Sara's hand. 'Do you think I should, Sara?'

Sara gave him an exasperated look. 'Yes, I do. You're always jumping to conclusions, where he's concerned!'

'I know, I know. But sometimes I've had cause. All right, Philip, I'll leave you with your patient!'

After he had gone Philip Landry looked down at Sara smilingly. 'Poor old J.K.,' he said sympathetically. 'You see, he and Jarrod are too much alike. They always have been. And I'm afraid J.K. judges Jarrod's reactions by what his own might have been at the same age.'

Sara allowed him to take her pulse. 'I don't think that's an entirely kind remark,' she murmured, with some amusement.

Doctor Landry laughed. 'You know,' he said, 'nor do I. However, do you know something? It was Jarrod who called the specialist in from London, against his father's better judgement. J.K. didn't at first think that was going to be necessary. But afterwards he realised that Jarrod had been right all along. After all, I'm just a country G.P., whereas Stafford Lonsdale is wholly concerned with pulmonary and respiratory diseases.'

'I see.'

'Naturally, he knew the best drugs to use and was able to get them. That's why your recovery has been so swift.'

Sara considered this. It was typical of Jarrod to want the best treatment available. He was impatient with incompetence. Even so, it was just another example of the way he arrogantly got what he wanted.

Within two weeks Sara was completely recovered, although her cheeks were not so round and there was no colour in them. The weather persisted in remaining cold and damp, and when it wasn't snowing, a thick mist shrouded the moors behind them, sweeping down on to the house constantly. J.K. got quite worried about her, particularly as she seemed without vitality, browsing about the house, reading and listening to records, but showing none of the youthful exuberance she had hitherto displayed.

Jarrod had not returned to Malthorpe. He had work to do in London, and instead he telephoned J.K. frequently, always asking about Sara's health, but making no attempt to discover for himself if she was all right.

Sara had plenty of telephone calls, boys she had met at Howard Lawson's party, trying to make dates with her, all of which she refused. Howard himself was the most persistent, once driving over to the Hall to see her, only to find a pale reflection of the girl he had enjoyed dancing with. Sara seemed uninterested in everything, and was not particularly tactful when turning down his invitation to take her to the theatre in Leeds. He went away rather annoyed, but Sara didn't seem to care, much to J.K.'s chagrin. He liked Howard, and had hoped Sara would make friends with him.

A month after the disastrous night she was taken ill, J.K. came to a decision. He told Sara about it while they were having dinner one evening.

'How would you like a couple of weeks in the West Indies?' he asked, surprising her tremendously.

Sara's eyes widened and then she dropped her gaze. 'Do you want to go there?' she asked, frowning. 'I should have thought you would rather go to the Continent.'

J.K. gave an impatient exclamation. 'What! With floods in Italy and France, and one of the coldest winters recorded behind them? No, Sara, the Continent just won't do!' He studied his soup with some intensity. 'Besides, I wasn't planning on taking you myself!' He sighed. 'You know what Philip's like, he's a bit of a worrier, and he doesn't recommend energetic pastimes like travel just now.'

Sara frowned. 'Then how?—oh, J.K., I'm not planning to go alone.'

J.K. sighed again. 'Stop jumping to conclusions, Sara! I wasn't suggesting that you should go alone. Heavens, if you were to go alone, you could stay a lot longer than a couple of weeks. But two weeks is all the time Jarrod can afford just now!'

'Jarrod!' Sara's eyes nearly popped out of her head. 'Jarrod! What has Jarrod got to do with it?'

'Well, everything, obviously. It was my idea, but he will take the responsibility!'

'Oh no! No!' Sara left the table somewhat jerkily. 'I don't want to go away with Jarrod. Besides, it wouldn't be right.'

'Why?'

'Well, I don't suppose he's all that keen.'

J.K. frowned. 'What Jarrod says about it is beside the point. It's the least he can do after what happened!'

Sara looked at him. 'Oh, J.K.! Have you asked him already?'

'Of course.'

Sara lifted her shoulders helplessly. 'What did you do that for, without telling me?'

'Well!' J.K.'s frown deepened. 'Quite honestly, Sara, you're worrying me. You mope around here all the time. You haven't even continued with your driving lessons! You refuse to go out with young Lawson, and you seem completely enervated. I realise that in addition to your illness you may be feeling more acutely now the absence of your grandfather, but nevertheless, the change will do you the world of good!'

Sara shook her head as Hester offered her the smoked salmon, and perched on the edge of the table in the corner. 'Well, really, it is just the after effects of my illness,' she protested. 'There's absolutely nothing wrong with me.'

'So you say. But I know this weather is depressing, and living here with an old man like me isn't exactly exciting. No'—he held his hand up when she began to protest—'no, Sara, you need a change of scenery, and Jamaica is a beautiful place.'

'Jamaica?'

'Of course. You'll stay with Jarrod's mother, naturally. Helen would be most upset if Jarrod went there and stayed anywhere else. Besides, the house she owns in the Blue Mountains has its own swimming pool, and the climate is marvellous at this time of the year.'

Sara felt her interest increasing in spite of herself. The prospect of spending two weeks with Jarrod had seemed exciting, but disturbing, and she was not altogether sure that such a prolonged period in his company would not arouse emotions inside her which she was desperately trying to subdue. She did not know why she felt this way; certainly Jarrod had never seemed at all interested in her—conversely in fact, she was a nuisance to be tolerated and nothing more.

But staying with his mother was different. She had plenty of natural curiosity, and she would like to meet the woman who had been J.K.'s wife.

'Well?' prompted J.K. 'What have you to say now?'

Sara sighed. 'I don't know what to say.'

'Do you want to go?'

Sara moved uncomfortably. 'Does Jarrod want to go, surely that's more to the point?'

'Any objections Jarrod may have are purely

95

selfish ones,' replied J.K., wiping his mouth with his table ·napkin. 'Don't concern yourself with Jarrod's affairs. Now, come and finish your dinner.'

When dinner was over Doctor Landry arrived to play chess with J.K. After having a glass of sherry with them, Sara left them to their game, wandering aimlessly about the house, restless and incapable of settling down with a book as she usually did.

Her mind was active with the problem of the proposed trip to Jamaica. She would not have been human had she not felt excited at the prospect of two weeks in the sun, away from the damp and cold of England at this time of the year. But she wished J.K. had mentioned it to her before asking Jarrod. She would have liked to have been there, to gauge his reactions to such a request. Of course, it must all have been done by telephone, Jarrod hadn't been near them for weeks.

She entered the library, closing the door and leaning against it. A huge fire burned in the grate as usual, and in the firelight the room looked warm and inviting. A cream telephone stood silently on the small bureau in the corner, and as her eyes flickered over it, an idea occurred to her. If she were to ring Jarrod herself, speak to him personally, she would be able to ask him about the trip, discover for herself what he had to say.

In theory it seemed a good idea, but in practice her nerves took over. Her voice trembled as she asked for the number, and her hand shook as she listened to the ringing tone. It seemed to ring for ages and ages before anyone answered it, and she was beginning to feel a sense of relief that he was not there, when the receiver was lifted and a woman's voice said the number. At first Sara thought she had a wrong number, but then she realised from the sounds of music and laughter that there must be a party going on, and that very likely the person who had answered was one of the maids. She was about to say it didn't matter, when she heard the woman say, to a third person:

'I don't know who it is, darling, they haven't answered yet. Perhaps they're in a coin box and haven't the change.'

Sara swallowed hard, felt a shiver run up her spine and then heard Jarrod say: 'Who is this?' in a short abrupt tone.

'It's me—Sara!' she managed, very quietly, and he said:

'Who? Sara? Oh, is something wrong, Sara? Is my father ill?' His voice was only slightly warmer.

'Er—no, Mr. Kyle, J.K. is fine.' Sara stumbled over the words, feeling awkward and immature. Was that woman, the one who had called Jarrod 'darling', still listening to their conversation?

'Then what is it, Sara?' There was the faintest sign of impatience now.

'I—I wanted to speak to you, Mr. Kyle,' she stammered. 'But—but—privately!'

'Look, Sara, there's a party going on here, I can't possibly have any lengthy discussions with you at this moment!' His attitude was wholly impatient now.

And as though his words triggered off some defence mechanism inside Sara, she felt her own anger rising. 'Oh, that's all right, Mr. Kyle,' she said coldly. 'Sorry I bothered you. Goodnight!' and she slammed down the receiver.

After she had done so, she felt contrite. After all, he was entertaining, and maybe she was being unreasonable ringing him at such a time and expecting him to speak to her, but then she hardened her heart as she remembered his cold impatience, and hunching her shoulders she moved closer to the fire. She would have to content herself with waiting until he decided he had time to visit them at Malthorpe.

She was startled out of her wits when the telephone started ringing. She rose at once to answer it, and then hesitated. It could be Jarrod! And if it were, she didn't want to speak to him. The effort of calling him in the first place had taken all her energies, and she was not willing to enter into any further arguments this evening.

The ringing stopped, and she realised that Morris or one of the servants had answered it. She relaxed, and lay back in her chair. She ought to be feeling happy and contented, living here in such luxury without a care in the world, yet all she felt was an emotional disorder that was heightened every time she considered going to Jamaica with a man who obviously found her nothing but an annoying responsibility.

The library door opened after a brief tap on its panels, and Morris stood there. 'Excuse me, Miss Sara,' he said, 'but Mr. Jarrod is calling you from London. Will you take the call in here?'

Sara jumped jerkily to her feet. 'Oh—oh yes, all right, Morris. Did—did he say why he was calling me?' She swallowed hard. 'Are you sure it's not J.K. he wants to speak to?'

Morris half-smiled. 'Definitely you, miss,' he replied kindly, as though aware of her discomfiture.

'Yes—yes, all right, Morris, thank you.' Sara gingerly lifted the telephone receiver from its cradle, and Morris withdrew, leaving her alone. 'He—hello, Sara Robins speaking.'

'Sara.' Jarrod's voice was taut. 'Don't ever hang up on me again!'

Sara shivered although the room was hot. 'I—I didn't hang up on you,' she protested, her anger again dissipated by nerves. 'You—you were obviously busy. I didn't want to trouble you any more.'

'Rubbish!' Jarrod sounded furious. 'Anyway, I'm alone now, for the moment at least, so let's have it. What do you want?'

Sara took a deep breath. 'I really want nothing at all, from you,' she replied stiffly. 'I—I had a notion to ask you about something, that was all. I realise I was stupid; it was not the time or the place. I guess it doesn't matter anyway.' This last was said rather pathetically.

Jarrod seemed to be controlling his temper with difficulty. 'Sara,' he began, 'I shan't ask you again! I want to know why you rang—now!'

Sara hesitated. 'Well, if you must have it, it's about this—this proposed trip J.K. has planned for Jamaica——'

'And?' he prompted impatiently.

'You don't want to take me!' It was a statement rather than a question.

'Did J.K. tell you that?'

'No. Not exactly. I guessed.'

'Did it ever occur to you that your unsophisticated attempts at estimating my opinion might be wrong?'

99

Sara sighed. 'J.K. ought not to have mentioned it to you without my knowledge. I don't want to feel beholden to you!'

Jarrod gave a short laugh. 'Don't you now? And don't your wardrobe, your car, and your present status make you feel beholden?'

Sara felt a hard lump in her throat. 'Th—that's a terrible thing to say!' she whispered, unable to find any healthy resentment inside her. 'Oh, how can you? How can you?' and with shaking fingers she replaced the receiver on its cradle, sitting staring at the telephone with tortured eyes. She had never felt so desolate, not even in those awful first days after her grandfather's sudden death. She had known Jarrod was hard and cynical, but he had never been so cruel to her before.

As before the telephone began to ring again, but Sara moved away from it, and when Morris tapped at the door to tell her that Jarrod wanted her again, she merely shook her head dumbly, forcing the unshed tears to remain stationary. She wouldn't—she couldn't speak to him again!

Morris gave up after a moment, and went away, but he came back again, looking concerned. 'Won't you please speak to Mr. Jarrod?' he asked. 'He is most insistent.'

'No—no, Morris. Tell him—tell him I've gone to bed.'

Morris sighed, and closed the door, and after a few minutes the door opened again, but this time it was J.K. He was frowning, and Sara sighed heavily.

'You've been speaking to Jarrod,' he said, looking intently at her. 'Did he ring you?'

'Yes—at least—oh, I suppose you already know anyway, I rang him first.' Sara hunched her shoulders.

'But why?'

'I wanted to ask him about the trip to Jamaica. I knew he didn't want to take me! Oh, J.K., I wish you hadn't asked him. He's too absorbed with his life here to want to take a stupid teenager to the West Indies! Then, when I rang, there was this party going on, and a woman answered, and Jarrod didn't want to speak to me, and I hung up on him, and he got mad——' Her voice trailed away, and she lifted her shoulders in an eloquent gesture. 'That's all!'

'All! All! Isn't that enough? Good lord, Sara, whatever possessed you to attempt to speak to him tonight? You might know he wouldn't be tactful. Jarrod seldom is. At least, so far as we are concerned.'

'Tactful!' Sara bit hard on her lower lip. 'He was horrible! Horrible!' She buried her face in her hands, the hot tears forcing their way between her fingers, and dropping into her lap.

'Oh, my dear!' J.K. went down on his haunches beside her. 'For heaven's sake, don't cry, darling! Jarrod didn't mean it, whatever he said. He might be cynical and selfish, but he's not intentionally cruel.'

'Isn't he?' She rubbed her eyes blindly. 'I think I hate him!'

'Don't be silly, Sara. Whatever did he say to upset you so?'

'I—I—I said I didn't want to feel beholden to him—for taking me to Jamaica, of course, and he said—he said—oh, he said I already was beholden to him—for—for everything!'

J.K. made a grunt of annoyance. 'Well, Sara,' he said, sighing, 'I suppose in a way you are. Did he say he wanted to be rid of that responsibility?'

Sara looked up. 'N-o,' she said slowly.

'Well, there you are then!'

'Oh, it's not as simple as that,' said Sara, taking out her handkerchief and drying her eyes. 'He doesn't have to say everything. I just *know*!'

'I think you're letting your imagination run away with you,' said J.K. firmly 'Now, come along, come and watch Doctor Landry get his just deserts. I've cornered him, and he can't possibly escape!' He smiled encouragingly.

Sara nodded, and allowed him to lead her from the room, but inwardly she was as distraught as before.

CHAPTER SIX

LATE that night, when Sara was lying sleeplessly in her comfortable bed, she heard the powerful roar of a car's engine coming up the drive. Immediately, her senses were vibrantly alive, as she realised it could only be Jarrod at this time of night. No one else would have been allowed through the gates, and she felt a quivering sensation in the pit of her stomach. Why had he come back so unexpectedly? Had he spoken to J.K.? And if so, what had been said?

Sliding out of bed, she slipped her arms into the sleeves of the amber-coloured quilted housecoat that lay at the foot of her bed. She had to be certain that it was Jarrod. She had to see him for herself to know he was actually there.

Opening her bedroom door, she stepped out on to the dimly lit landing, padding silently along to where the balcony fell away into the beautiful well of the hall. A lamp glowed on a polished chest in the hall, illuminating the heavy door, and casting a mellow glow on the dark carpet. Outside, she could hear a wind moaning through the trees, and the silence was almost tangible.

Then a car door slammed, and a few moments later a key was inserted in the door, and it swung inwards to admit Jarrod. Dressed in a dark overcoat over a dark suit, the swarthy cast of his tan made a vivid contrast to the lightness of his hair. Tall, and lean, moving with the smooth, lithe grace of a predator, he epitomised all that was sleek and powerful and disturbing to Sara, and she pressed a hand to her lips as she realised the emotions he aroused in her were not at all as simple as hatred. In all her young life she had never wanted to touch a man, never experienced a sensual awareness of her own body and its needs and desires, never imagined in her wildest dreams that she might find herself physically attracted to a man twice her age. Yet she was; there was no denying it now that she had seen him again, and she needed time to assimilate her feelings. She was not in love with him—love wasn't like this. Love was a gentle thing that grew with warmth and affection, not this vibrating turmoil that desired a satisfaction that was wholly alien to her. She could understand at least now how Lauren must feel, if she was attracted to Jarrod. Knowing he met a lot of women, this Tracy Merrick in particular, knowing he was fully capable of satisfying his senses without any lasting ties, must be a tortuous experience.

Sara turned her back on the scene down in the hall as Jarrod shed his overcoat, and flicked through the small pile of mail that awaited him on the hall salver. She would not think about it any more; she would put it right out of her mind. She would not allow herself to think of him in this way. It was senseless, it was stupid—it was degrading! He was only a man!

Wrapping her housecoat about her, she smoothed her hair, and turned to make her way back to her bedroom. But she had not been conscious of the swift passage of time and in those few moments she had taken to gather her emotions, Jarrod had mounted the stairs and now stood regarding her cynically some two feet away.

'Oh!' Sara gasped in astonishment.

'Good evening, Sara,' he said sardonically. 'How nice of you to provide a welcoming committee!'

'I didn't—I mean—excuse me!' She would have brushed past him, but he halted her easily, his fingers about her small wrist.

'Don't go,' he mocked her, 'you and I haven't finished our conversation!'

'We—we can't discuss anything tonight,' she said, trembling in his grasp. 'Please let me go—I don't want to arouse your father by having to shout for help!'

'What makes you think I might do something to make you want to shout for help?' he murmured huskily, regarding her rather more intently, making Sara acutely conscious of the scarcity of her attire. With her hair loose about her shoulders, she was unaware of the elusive quality of her allure, but Jarrod was aware of it, his own senses heightened by their argument earlier, and the violent, savage journey he had made from London, as much in contrition as anger.

'Nothing—nothing!' Sara felt a breathless inertia overtaking her. It was so late, and the wind outside isolated them from the rest of the world, and her own thoughts of a few minutes ago were still very much uppermost in her mind. Jarrod was very close, and she could smell the clean male smell about him combined with cigar smoke and a faint odour of brandy. She was fast losing the urge to escape from him, and she wondered what he would do if instead of trying to draw away she moved closer to him so that he was completely aware of her.

Jarrod was aware of the moment, too. His eyes were no longer mocking but warm and disturbing, the sensual curve of his mouth an indication of his emotions. He slid his fingers up her wrist, over her forearm to her shoulder, and taking a strand of her hair in his fingers, twined it round his hand. His eyes held hers, only occasionally shifting to her mouth so that Sara almost felt that he had caressed her.

'Jarrod,' she murmured achingly, longing for the fulfilment of passion, when he tugged his hand savagely away from her hair, causing her to wince in pain as he made for the head of the stairs.

'Go to bed, Sara,' he said harshly.

She stared at him without speaking, hugging herself shakily, and he swore violently. 'For God's sake, Sara, go to bed, before I change my mind!'

She stared at him for a moment longer, and then without a word sped along the corridor to her room, opening her door with trembling fingers, closing it behind her, and almost convulsively turning the key in the lock for the first time. Then she went to the mirror, gazing at herself with agonised eyes, seeing the hurt and bewilderment mirrored there. Oh God, she thought, shivering uncontrollably, what have I done? *What have I done?*

When she went down to breakfast next morning there were dark rings round her eyes, and J.K. who was sitting reading a newspaper with his coffee, frowned when he noticed them. 'Didn't you sleep?' he asked bluntly.

Sara seated herself before replying. 'Not—not very well,' she murmured. 'I—well, the wind was very strong.'

J.K. looked sceptical, and then, pouring himself another cup of coffee, he said: 'Jarrod arrived last night.'

Sara controlled her colour with difficulty. 'Oh—oh, did he?' she said, sipping her fruit juice. 'Did you know he was coming?'

'Not really, although I suspected he might after your argument on the phone last evening. No matter how you see it, Jarrod is not vindictive. He probably needs to apologise. Besides, it will give us the ideal opportunity to discuss this trip. I thought you might leave at the end of the week.'

'At the end of the week?' Sara's eyes were wide. 'But—but we couldn't—we couldn't possibly!'

'Why not? You know you obtained your passport weeks ago. There's absolutely nothing to stop you. Jarrod is perfectly well aware of the proximity of the departure date.'

Sara felt all traces of appetite leaving her. She couldn't go abroad with Jarrod right now, not immediately. She needed time to think, to gather together her scattered senses, to get things into perspective, to achieve that detached aloofness that would prevent her from making a complete fool of herself.

'Where—where is Jarrod?' she asked in a small voice.

'He went out about six-thirty—on Alexander. It's quite a bracing morning, for all the cold, and I expect he'll ride over to the Maxwells' for breakfast.'

'Oh.' She finished her fruit juice. 'What—what

did he say?'

'Nothing much. Why?' J.K. regarded her speculatively. 'He can't have slept much last night. He didn't get here until after midnight—much later than that, actually, and to be out so early . . . ' He shrugged. 'Maybe his conscience is troubling him.'

Sara doubted this, particularly after the incident on the upper landing. At the remembrance of this the colour flooded her cheeks, and J.K. narrowed his eyes. 'Don't let Jarrod hurt you,' he said, surprisingly. 'His bark is much worse than his bite.'

She managed a half-smile. 'Do you think so? Oh, J.K., I wish you hadn't decided on this trip to Jamaica! It will be impossible!'

J.K. sighed. 'Look, Sara, you're only travelling with Jarrod. When you get there, Helen will be your hostess, and she'll see that you're not left a target for Jarrod's ill-humour. Besides, Jarrod likes Jamaica, and I daresay you may find him a much more agreeable person away from my influence.'

'You never said a truer word!' a cool, amused voice remarked, and Sara glanced round, startled, to find Jarrod leaning against the door post. 'What a cosy chat you seem to be having,' he remarked, with some dryness. 'The trials and errors of life in a goldfish bowl!'

'Don't be so sarcastic, Jarrod,' said J.K. sharply. 'Where's Lauren? I would have thought you would be breakfasting there if you'd been riding with her.'

Jarrod flung himself into a seat at the table, pouring himself some coffee. 'I have not been riding with Lauren, I haven't even seen Lauren,' he replied sardonically. 'I preferred my own company this morning.' His eyes flickered over Sara swiftly, and she bent her head to avoid the speculation in his gaze. 'Do you not ride these days, Sara?'

'No.' Sara was abrupt.

'Sara hasn't done anything since her illness,' replied J.K. 'I believe I told you several times, she's not well, at least she hasn't recovered her spirits since her weeks in bed. This is my dilemma, the reason I asked you to take the trouble to take her to Jamaica!'

Jarrod studied Sara's bent head. 'How do you feel about it, Sara?' he asked.

Sara looked up, then applied her attention to her toast. 'As I told you last night, I have no desire to be an encumbrance to you. Maybe I am looking rather washed out, but it will pass. As soon as the weather gets warmer, I shall be fine!'

'No, you will not!' thundered J.K. 'Not sufficiently fast for me, at any rate. Jarrod, tell the child you'll take her to your mother's with good grace! Don't make her feel such a nuisance!'

Jarrod raised his dark eyebrows. 'Did I say that? Did I say she was a nuisance?'

'You apparently said enough,' retorted J.K. 'You're so wrapped up in your own blasted affairs that you have no time to think of anyone but yourself!'

'Oh, please!' Sara rose to her feet. 'Don't, please, have any more argument over me! I've told you, I don't want to go to Jamaica!'

Jarrod rose too, towering over her, making her acutely conscious of him. 'Of course you want to go,' he said smoothly. 'And what's more you're going! The arrangements are already made. This morning I telephoned the agency I deal with in London, advising them of my requirements!'

Sara stared at him. 'But you couldn't possibly. It's only nine-fifteen now. Agencies don't open before nine.'

Jarrod gave a short laugh. 'My dear Sara, when you're the chairman of a combine like Kyle Textiles there is no such word as *don't*. The manager of the agency, Robert Leyton, would open his office at two o'clock in the morning if I asked him!'

Sara compresed her lips. 'Oh really,' she said bitterly. 'You're so sure, aren't you, so confident, so arrogant! You can't believe that I might not *want* to go with you to Jamaica!'

'Frankly no. Oh, I don't flatter myself it's my company you're wanting, but you did say you wanted to travel, didn't you, and I'm sure such an opportunity could not go unnoticed!'

'Jarrod! For God's sake——' J.K. smote his fist on the table. 'She's no match for you, and that tongue of yours. Leave her alone! You say you've made arrangements for the flight?'

Jarrod looked round at his father. 'Yes. Matt is going with us.'

'Matt?' J.K. frowned. 'Why?'

'I decided he should.' Jarrod was non-committal.

'When did you decide this?'

'This morning, actually. Any objections?'

Sara sighed. Who was this Matt they were talking about? And why was he going to Jamaica with Jarrod? Had it anything to do with the abandoned way she had acted the previous evening? She had been so wrapped up in her own feelings she had not stopped to think how Jarrod might construe her actions.

J.K. seemed to sense the trend of her thoughts, and he said: 'John Matthews, Matt, as we call him, is Jarrod's personal assistant, as well as being a close friend. He's nice, you'll like him. Jarrod, are you taking the direct flight?'

'No. We leave Saturday morning and stay overnight in New York. The flight to Kingston leaves Sunday afternoon.'

'I see. What do you intend doing in New York? I suppose it's not just by chance that you're staying there overnight.'

'Well,' Jarrod thrust his hands into the pockets of his pants, 'I thought I might get to meet Jefferson Saturday evening.'

J.K. clicked his tongue in annoyance. 'Jarrod, this is not to be an excuse for a business trip.'

'J.K.,' Jarrod's voice was equally hard, 'I make my own rules, and I play by them. Don't try altering the game, because your rules just don't apply!'

J.K. sighed. 'I'd be interested to know exactly what your game is, Jarrod,' he said dryly.

Jarrod smiled. 'I guess you would at that,' he conceded. 'I suppose Sara feels the same way. However,' as Sara walked to the door, 'this is not the time, or the place, for inquisitions on my character. Well, Sara, can you be ready in three days, do you suppose? Potter can bring you down to London on Friday, and you can stay overnight at my apartment.' He gave his father a wry glance. 'I'll ask Tracy to stay there, too.' He looked back at Sara. 'Just so everything is proper.'

J.K. nodded decisively. 'All right, Jarrod. Sara can manage that. I'll see she does.'

Sara heaved a sigh. It seemed she had no choice but to give in with good grace. After all, with this Matt along, it would relieve matters, and there would be no intimate moments alone with Jarrod.

'I—I think I'll go and wash my hair,' she said now, excusing herself, and J.K. frowned.

'You're not brooding?'

'No, of course not.'

'Good,' said Jarrod. 'Because I'm leaving again this afternoon, and I'd hate to feel you were annoyed with me!'

'My opinion of you can hardly matter one iota,' returned Sara, with some anoyance, hardly able to credit that that little scene on the upper landing had ever occurred. Jarrod, this mocking, sardonic man, could never have looked at *her* with such melting warmth, never triggered off such an explosion of dangerous awareness between them; it just was not possible.

As she left the room, Jarrod said: 'I'll see you at lunch, I expect, but if not Friday afternoon, right?'

'Right,' responded Sara, somewhat wearily, and did not bother to look back at him again. She wanted to get away quite badly, and try and retrieve her lost defences.

Ventura Court was a tall, imposing block of luxury apartments, favoured by businessmen, television personnel and personalities from the entertainment world. Here they lived in isolated anonymity, in opulent surroundings, separated from the pressures of the outside world by a very capable commissionaire and two porters who resembled retired wrestlers.

To Sara, it looked cold and uninviting, and although the evening was warmer, and a faint sun was setting as Potter brought the limousine to a halt by the shallow flight of steps that led up to the swing glass doors, she shivered quite uncontrollably, as much from nerves as anything else. She looked down at the orange slack suit she was wearing with some misgivings. Combined with her auburn hair and creamy complexion, it was very attractive, but she felt overdressed and uncomfortable, wishing herself miles away from here.

Potter opened the door, revealed his identity to the commissionaire, and then escorted her up in the lift, with her cases, to the penthouse apartment that Jarrod occupied. The lift doors opened on to a thickly carpeted hallway, and Potter led the way to the double white doors with KYLE written on them in tiny gold letters.

'Well, miss,' he said, as he rang the bell, 'here we are! I hope you're going to have an enjoyable holiday in Jamaica. I envy you, I really do.'

Sara half-smiled, a trifle wanly. 'Believe me, Potter, if I could change places with you, I would.'

Potter looked taken aback, and she thought she ought not to have said anything so revealing to a chauffeur of J.K.'s. Still, Potter was more like a friend, and he had known she had left rather distressed at leaving J.K. behind. He had looked so lonely, standing on the steps of Malthorpe Hall, and she had wanted to stop the car and dash back to the security of his arms. Somehow, even with her grandfather, who had been an undemonstrative man at best, she had never felt the same sense of

113

belonging, and in a short time J.K. had come to mean a lot to her.

Now the doors of the apartment were opened, and another manservant stood there.

'This is Hastings,' said Potter, in explanation to Sara. 'Hastings, this is Miss Sara Robins, Mr. Jarrod is expecting her.'

'Oh yes, Potter,' Hastings nodded, and smiled. He was a little like Morris, Sara thought, and she later discovered that they were cousins. 'Come in, miss. Mr. Jarrod isn't in at the moment, but Miss Merrick is here, waiting to greet you.'

Immediately Sara's heart sank to her shoes. Another obstacle to meet and overcome! If only Jarrod had allowed her to arrive and make herself at home alone. As it was she was to meet yet another edition of Lauren Maxwell, all ready to make a verbal meal of her. She didn't know whether she would be able to stand it.

Potter left her in the wide entrance hall that was hung with chandeliers, and resembled a small drawing-room with its upholstered chairs and table. Then Sara was helped out of the dark cape she was wearing over her suit, and Hastings invited her to follow him.

They descended two steps to a low hall that ran the length of the apartment. Doors opened to right and left, and Hastings advised her that Miss Merrick would show her her room later. Then he opened the door into a long low lounge, carpeted in scarlet and royal blue, with white chairs and couches, upholstered in real skin. The walls were cream and hung with vivid sketches and paintings and plaques, that gave it an exciting exotic appearance. The lighting was all concealed apart from a couple of standard lamps, very modern things with many branches, while one wall was almost entirely made of glass, hung with an enormous venetian blind that was flicked open giving a panoramic view of the lights of London below.

A girl had been fiddling around with a huge television set in one corner, but she jumped to her feet at their entrance, and turned to greet them. Sara had an impression of a cap of silvery blonde hair, slanted blue eyes and a very short red evening dress before the girl came gracefully across to meet them on slender legs. She was tall and very thin, but very elegant.

'Hello, Sara,' she said, smiling warmly. 'I'm Tracy Merrick, but just call me Tracy, everyone does. Hastings, can we have some ice, love? There isn't any in the container.'

Hastings nodded smilingly, and then left them alone. Dazedly Sara smiled her own greeting, and then Tracy drew her across to a low couch, and said: 'Come and sit down, and get warm, and tell me all about yourself. Jarrod said you were only seventeen, is that right? How marvellous! When you get to my age you begin to realise how old twenty-five can really be!'

Sara began to relax. Tracy was not at all like Lauren. For all her assumed air of sophistication, she was not very different from herself, with an easy outgoing manner, that held none of Lauren's bored indifference.

'Twenty-five isn't old,' she protested, and Tracy laughed.

'Well, sometimes I feel old,' she confessed. 'Men

are so much luckier than women. They don't age half so much, and a man in his thirties is so much more exciting than a woman of the same age. Anyway, at least you don't have to worry about that. When are you eighteen, by the way?'

'In a little over ten days,' said Sara, brightening. 'It seems to have come round so fast, I can hardly believe it.'

'Oh, the beginning of April. My birthday is in July. I shall be twenty-six then, worse luck. But enough of that. Are you looking forward to going to Jamaica?'

Sara hesitated. 'Well, I suppose I am. But—well, I wish J.K. could have taken me.'

'Who? Oh yes, Jarrod's father. Why? Don't you like Jarrod?'

Sara flushed. 'Well, yes, but—oh, I don't know. I'm sure he doesn't want to take me—he'd much rather stay here with his—his friends. Like—like yourself, for example.'

'Oh, Jarrod sees plenty of us, I can assure you. He and Daddy are great friends, and naturally he's often at our house. He's known me since I was your age, of course, and I absolutely adore him. He's the most marvellous companion. I'm sure you'll have great fun in Jamaica. Get Jarrod to take you skin-diving, and water-skiing. He's fabulously good.'

Tracy's whole conversation seemed to be interspersed by words like 'fabulous' and 'marvellous', and later 'terrific', and Sara began to think that perhaps Tracy was a little young for her age. But she was very kind and very friendly, and Sara soon lost her own inhibitions and they chatted together like old friends, Sara telling her all about her life with her grandfather, and now with J.K. When a key inserted in the door announced the arrival home of Jarrod Kyle, Sara almost felt disappointed, and Tracy jumped to her feet and ran to meet him welcomingly, revealing more potently than words could say just how she felt about him.

Jarrod was still in the hall, removing his overcoat, and Sara heard him say: 'Not now, Tracy! Is Sara here?'

Tracy said: 'Oh, Jarrod, you are a pig! Yes, of course Sara's here! We've been having a long interesting conversation!' She preceded him into the lounge, and Sara forced herself to remain seated when all her being longed to remove itself as far from Jarrod Kyle as the room allowed.

Jarrod looked at her with narrowed eyes, taking in the attractive picture she made in the orange suit, jacket removed to reveal a royal blue slim-fitting roll-collared sweater, her long hair tumbling in disorder about her shoulders, her cheeks flushed from the sherry Tracy had provided her with.

'Well, Sara,' he said, bowing his head slightly, 'have you made yourself at home? How do you like my small abode?'

'Small!' Sara ran her tongue over her lips. 'It's hardly that, is it? But I like it.'

'Oh, praise indeed,' he exclaimed, bowing mockingly again. 'Did you hear that, Tracy? The child likes it.'

'Not so much of the child, Jarrod,' returned Tracy defensively. 'Sara's having a birthday in eleven days' time. While you're out there in the sun! Her eighteenth!'

'It that so?' Jarrod frowned. 'I must try and remember.'

'I shouldn't bother,' murmured Sara, almost in-
audibly, but he grinned at her, and she knew he had
heard every word.

They dined soon afterwards, and then Jarrod
said: 'I think you ought to have an early night,
Sara. We have to be out to the airport for seven in
the morning.'

Tracy frowned at him. 'And are you having an
early night, too?'

Sara thought this was highly unlikely. Very much
more likely was the idea that she should retire
leaving Tracy and himself alone. However, she was
wrong, for Jarrod said:

'I have to go out and see Matt. He's meeting us
at the airport, but there are various things that have
to be tied up at the office. However, I'm sure an
early night won't do you any harm, Tracy.'

Tracy now looked a little put out for the first
time. 'I'm not a child, Jarrod. Can't I go with you?
Surely what you have to do won't take that long?
Heavens, my being here in the first place is so
ridiculous! Only J.K. would think of something like
this. You're almost old enough to be Sara's father,
does he honestly imagine you're not to be trusted!'

Jarrod's expression was hard now. 'He didn't
imagine anything, Tracy. Your presence here was
my idea. I don't want Sara's reputation jeopardised
because she has to spend a night in my apartment.'

Tracy grimaced. 'Why should it be? Are you
afraid you might make violent passionate love to
her if I'm not here to restrain you?' She laughed
harshly, and Sara felt something inside her curl up

and die. Tracy wasn't so different from Lauren after all, only her approach was different!

'I—I would like to go to bed,' she said awkwardly.

Jarrod rose from his place at the table. 'All right. I'll take you.'

'I thought—I mean—Hastings said——' Sara's voice trailed away.

'Come along,' said Jarrod firmly, taking her arm. Tracy lit another cigarette, regarding them both moodily, and Sara sighed. Oh, I wish this holiday was over, she thought longingly.

Her room was large, not so large as her room at Malthorpe, but equally luxurious, with a white carpet, white walls, and hangings and bedcovers of green and blue. The adjoining bathroom was also green-tiled and marble-floored, with a bath large enough for three people.

'I have no servants here, to speak of,' remarked Jarrod dryly. 'Hastings attends to all my needs, so I'm afraid you'll have to run your own bath and lay out your own clothes.'

'I—I can manage,' said Sara, nodding uncomfortably.

'For heaven's sake,' he exclaimed, 'stop acting so nervously. I'm quite harmless, really.'

Sara stiffened her shoulders. 'I never imagined you were anything else,' she denied, and turned her back on him.

'No, but your opinion of me hasn't improved with age. Why? What have I done, apart from having a few altercations with you?'

'Nothing—nothing.' Sara hunched her shoulders. 'Now I'd like to go to bed.'

'Would you? Very well, go to bed. I shall be back

later. Tracy will still be here if you need anything.'

Sara glanced round, unable to resist saying: 'Will she be waiting up for you?'

His eyes narrowed. 'Just what do you mean by that?'

Sara flushed. 'Nothing.'

'Not much! Heavens, what do you imagine we do—sleep together?' He gave a short mirthless laugh. 'Contrary to your beliefs, I do sleep alone sometimes!'

Sara allowed her eyes to rest on him for an insolent moment. 'How very unenterprising of you!' she remarked, and without waiting for his angry retaliation, she disappeared inside the bathroom, locking the door with an unusual sense of satisfaction. Nevertheless, it was some time before she ventured out again, only to find he had gone, the door closed quietly behind him.

CHAPTER SEVEN

THE journey to Jamaica was not the ordeal Sara had expected it to be. To begin with John Matthews, Matt, was one of the nicest men she had ever met, and he provided a buffer between herself and Jarrod. Not that one was really needed. From the moment the plane left Heathrow Jarrod seemed absorbed in his own affairs, studying a file of papers he had brought with him, and only occasionally discussing different aspects of it with Matt. They spent Saturday night in New York, Matt providing Sara with an evening meal while Jarrod took himself off to the New York Hilton to meet Charles Jefferson, a business colleague. After dinner, Matt took Sara for a taxi ride through the fastest living city in the world, but she was unimpressed by the claustrophobic height of the buildings, and the hustle and bustle on the streets below. Sunday morning Matt took her to Central Park, and then after a hasty lunch they boarded yet another plane which landed at the International Airport at Montego Bay at seven-thirty in the evening.

Even so, it was Sara's first taste of real luxury travelling. She had never known such deference from servants, stewardesses, hoteliers; a deference which Jarrod accepted with casual indifference, and which even Matt didn't seem to find at all surprising. Nevertheless, Sara appreciated the quality of her seat on each of the planes, snuggled down in the softness of her bed at the hotel in New York, and luxuriated in the depth of the baths that were run for her.

As it was dark when they arrived, she had no sense of her surroundings, and Matt said consolingly: 'The view from the terrace of Flamingo Lodge is almost an aerial one of the coastline below, and tomorrow morning you'll see for yourself what I mean.'

The International Airport was like all international airports, air-conditioned and impersonal, and it wasn't until they emerged from the airport buildings on to the tarmac that Sara realised just how far from London they had come. The velvet warmth of the night air was sweet-scented and buzzing with sounds and vibrations, entirely alien to her. To her surprise, they had not collected their luggage, and she caught Matt's arm, and said: 'Where are we going now?'

Jarrod glanced round with a lazy expression. 'We haven't finished with aeroplanes yet, Sara. Now we take the flight to Kingston. Only this time it's a little different.'

Sara frowned, and Matt grinned. 'He means it's not a scheduled trip,' he elucidated. 'This time we have no professional pilot.'

'Whatever do you mean?' Sara felt her stomach churning. So far she had not been air-sick, but her nerves were causing butterflies to disturb her stomach now.

Jarrod looked a little bored. 'He means, Sara, that it's my plane. I'm the pilot!'

'What!' Sara looked horrified, and Jarrod sighed heavily.

'Oh hell, what did you have to tell her for?' he asked Matt with some annoyance. 'We'd have boarded the plane, and she wouldn't have known until we were airborne. As it is she'll probably panic herself into something nauseating!'

Sara stiffened angrily. 'Don't you dare speak to me like that,' she exclaimed. 'I'm perfectly all right, and I intend to stay that way, whoever is handling the aircraft!'

'Good girl!' said Matt, laughing. 'Take no notice of Jarrod. He's only kidding!'

Sara doubted this, and her nerves were further increased by the discovery that the plane they were to use, Jarrod's plane, was a small jet, powerful and fast, and nothing like the twin-engined craft she had schooled herself to expect.

She was helped inside, to discover that the interior resembled a small lounge, comfortably furnished with armchairs and tables, a cocktail cabinet occupying one corner, and a bookcase the other. There was even a small film projector, which Matt explained was merely an added luxury and seldom used. Jarrod's compartment, at the front of the plane, was twin-seated, and she wondered what it would be like to fly beside him. However, she was strapped into one of the armchairs, while Matt occupied another, and Jarrod shed his jacket, and seated himself behind the controls. He was cleared for take-off, and with only the faintest sensations of speed the plane left the ground as smoothly as the huge liner had done. Matt released his strap and helped Sara to release hers, and then went to prepare some drinks. During their speedy passage through Customs, and afterwards, their cases had been installed aboard the plane, and Sara thought this was yet another example of the things Jarrod, and his contemporaries, took for granted. She was tremendously thrilled, and her butterflies disappeared with a welcoming sense of well-being that flooded through her being. After all, here she was, flying across one of the most beautiful areas in the world, in company with two attractive men, with the prospect of two weeks' holiday before her, with absolutely nothing to do but take it easy and recover her health and spirits. In such surroundings, she could not go on feeling depressed. J.K. had been right as usual, the trip was going to do her good.

She accepted a mixed fruit drink from Matt, and then accompanied him when he took Jarrod a tall glass of whisky and soda to the front compartment.

Jarrod glanced round and saw her, as he lit a cigar, and said: 'How do you feel now? Queasy?'

'Of course not,' she said, allowing a smile to play around her lips. 'Actually, I'm beginning to feel much better. Mentally, at least.'

Jarrod raised his dark eyebrows, and then looked at Matt. 'It must be your company, friend,' he said lazily, 'mine has never achieved that effect.'

Sara flushed, and as though repenting, he said: 'Come on, kid, come and sit down here, and take a look at the control panel. It's a pity it's not daylight, but still, I'll take you up another day. See, this is the altimeter, and the fuel gauge, and that's the radar system.'

Sara was fascinated. She was not particularly mechanically minded, but Jarrod explained everything so carefully that she found herself interested in spite of herself. It semed fantastic to imagine they were flying thousands of feet up in the atmosphere, talking casually like this as though discussing the state of the weather. Jarrod went on to tell her about hurricanes, and tornadoes, and to her astonishment she found herself completely fascinated, her eyes watching his long slender hands as he elaborated some facet of his story. She had never known he was so conversant with things outside the concrete world of his office building, and she felt ashamed that she had ever attempted to find the man behind the computer. That he had an intelligent brain she had never been in any doubt, his prowess in the business world had proved that, but this was an entirely different angle on his character. Maybe J.K. had been right again, maybe Jarrod was a better person away from his influence. At any rate, the half-hour journey was over in a flash, and soon the brilliant collection of lights below them heralded their arrival at Palisadoes, the airport which served the southern part of Jamaica and Kingston. Sara thought she had never seen a sky of that particular shade of deep blue, a kind of purplish quality, that shimmered like rich cloth set with jewels.

The landing was accomplished smoothly, and she realised afresh what a complex person Jarrod was. His handling of the plane had proved he was no amateur and yet he seemed unaffected and unassuming of his skill. It brought excited awareness of him bubbling to the surface of her being, and with it the knowledge that prolonged periods in his company could be more intoxicating than alcohol. A frightening thought to a girl without any experience of handling a man like that.

Palisadoes was some distance from Kingston, but when Custom formalities were over Sara found a huge Negro manservant awaiting them with a low-slung cream limousine that she suspected was a Cadillac. He took charge of the luggage helped by one of the airport porters, and gave Jarrod a welcoming grin that conveyed very clearly how glad he was to see him again.

'This is Aristotle,' remarked Jarrod, flinging his overcoat over one shoulder, and running a lazy hand through his hair. 'He's chauffeur-cum-handy-man-cum-bodyguard to my mother.'

Sara glanced at him. 'Surely your mother doesn't need a bodyguard!' she exclaimed in alarm.

Matt grinned now. 'Take no notice of him, Sara,' he said, 'Aristotle has many duties, but bodyguarding is not one of them.'

'No, but he could be,' returned Jarrod easily, and Sara relaxed. She was unused to this new lazy side of Jarrod Kyle.

They left the airport behind them swiftly, and Sara glanced back out of the rear window, seeing the lights disappearing into the darkness. Matt sat beside her in the back, while Jarrod himself drove with Aristotle beside him. Their conversation was about the weather, the swimming, the fishing and the golf, and as far as Sara could gather Aristotle accompanied Jarrod almost everywhere while he was in Jamaica.

They were climbing now, away from the coastline which could faintly be discerned on the horizon, and Sara felt a surge of excitement enveloping her. This was a whole new world, a world she had not even known existed, and she felt determined to gain as much from it as she possibly could. This was no time for self-analysis and recriminations, she must live each day as it came, and enjoy it to the best of her ability.

The scents of the air were all new to her, and in the glow of the headlights the creamy petals of magnolia could be seen growing in wild profusion.

Matt glanced at Sara, sensing her animation. 'Excited?' he asked indulgently.

Sara smiled. 'Oh yes. I wasn't—when we left London—but now I am.'

Jarrod glanced round, but she could not see his expression in the gloom. 'It's like I said, Matt, you've worked the miracle.'

Sara was glad he could not see the hot colour run up her cheeks. 'No,' she said, unable to prevent the words. 'It's not only Matt!'

'Well, thanks!' said Matt in mock derision.

'No, really, you know what I mean, it's the feel of the place. Can't you feel it?' she appealed to them. 'I mean, it's all so—so—different!'

'The pull of the islands,' remarked Jarrod, a trifle sardonically.

'Well, yes.'

'And all that goes with it, I suppose. Witchcraft, voodoo, black magic!'

'Don't be so sarcastic! You must know what I mean.'

'Okay,' he said lazily. 'Yes, I guess I do. It used to effect me that way, too. Say, Aristo, do we have some equipment for Sara to go skin-diving?'

Sara shivered. 'Skin-diving!' she exclaimed breathlessly.

'Sure. You'd like to do that, wouldn't you?'

'Oh yes, but—well, I don't know how!'

'Mr. Jarrod, he'll show you fine,' said Aristotle complacently. 'There's a cove, Devil's Point, you like that fine!'

Jarrod grinned, his white teeth visible in the gloom. 'Sure, she'll like it fine, Aristo,' he agreed, and Sara thought she would, too.

Flamingo Lodge was approached up a steep incline. The wrought iron gates stood wide, much different, Sara thought, from the almost hermit-like seclusion of Malthorpe Hall. A drive twisted among giant ceiba trees and cedars, ferns and flowers giving the grounds an almost jungle-like density. Then the floodlit front terrace of the lodge was visible, and Sara caught her breath at the beauty of its vine-hung verandas and balconies, all flowering colour and tracery. Shrubs spilled over the veranda steps, jasmine and jacaranda, hibiscus and frangipani, in brilliant shades that caught the light and threw it back in delicate prisms of colour. The perfumes of the night air were intensified, and mingled with them was the faintest trace of the salty tang of the sea, and a breeze lifted Sara's hair with blessed coolness. Her slack suit was not the most suitable attire for a summer evening in the semi-tropical climate of Kingston, but New York had been cold and damp and she had not thought to change on the plane.

The Cadillac halted, and Jarrod slid out, holding forward the front seat and giving his hand to Sara to help her to alight. Immediately at his touch she was aware of him, and she drew her hand swiftly away, willing her irresponsible senses to remain dormant.

A woman was coming down the veranda steps to greet them, a tall woman, with curly fair hair that framed her youthful face. She was obviously Jarrod's mother; it wasn't so much her looks, but the way she moved, and the slightly arrogant way she held her head. She looked at her son with warm, welcoming eyes, and although she didn't immediately fling her arms around him and make an enormous fuss of him, it was obvious that they understood one another, and each other's feelings.

'Hello, Helen,' said Jarrod, kissing her cheek. 'How have you been?'

'Oh, I'm perfectly well,' she said, smiling at him. 'How's J.K.?'

Sara thought it was significant that her first question should be about her husband. It proved Helen was not as indifferent to him as J.K. would have her believe.

Jarrod reassured her about J.K.'s health, adding that his heart was playing him up ever so slightly, and then drawing Sara forward, he said: 'This is Sara. I guess you know all about her.'

Helen Kyle studied Sara for a moment, and then said: 'Yes, I suppose I do. You're J.K.'s latest acquisition, I hear—or perhaps I ought to say Jarrod's.' She glanced at her son wryly, and Sara didn't know how to reply. However, Helen continued: 'I'm very pleased to have you here, Sara. You're more than welcome. If it means having my son back with me for two more weeks, I could love you for it!' She took Sara's hand warmly. 'Did you have a good journey?'

Sara relaxed a little. 'Marvellous, thank you.

Particularly the final stage.' She looked defiantly at Jarrod. 'I didn't know—Mr. Kyle—could pilot a plane, much less a jet!'

Helen frowned, and then gave Matt a brief greeting. 'You surely don't call Jarrod Mr. Kyle, do you?' she exclaimed. 'Heavens, I'm sure you call J.K. by that abbreviation, don't you?'

'Well, yes, I do,' admitted Sara, feeling tense again.

Jarrod mounted the steps to the veranda where a coloured maidservant was standing waiting. Handing his coat to the girl, he said: 'Come on in, for heaven's sake, Helen. I'm sure Sara's name for me is not important. At least to me, it's not. Now, I need a drink. Tell me, Sophie, have you mixed the Martinis as I like them?'

He disappeared inside, followed by Matt, and Helen said: 'Forgive me for catechising you like this. It's just that I feel so out of touch here, and I'd hate to feel that there were circumstances attached to this affair that I didn't understand.'

'What do you mean, Mrs. Kyle?' Sara's voice was taut.

Helen shook her head. 'As I understand it Jarrod is your guardian, is that right?' Sara nodded her assent, and Helen went on: 'But J.K. has taken it upon himself to take Jarrod's place. Why?'

'You must know it was J.K. who knew my grandfather.'

'Yes, of course,' Helen nodded. 'I was forgetting for the moment. Whenever I've spoken to Jarrod about it, he has considered you very much his responsibility!'

Sara swallowed hard. 'You've *spoken* to Jarrod!'

She frowned. 'About me?'

'Of course. There are such things as telephones, even here,' remarked Helen dryly, and Sara flushed. 'But come along. I'm being very rude keeping you standing out here like this. It's just that Jarrod is very dear to me, and I know he won't allow me to offer *him* any advice.'

Sara bit her lip. 'You—you want to offer me advice, Mrs. Kyle?'

Helen shook her head again. 'No. No, not now. Not now I've met you. I can see for myself that you're little more than a child, and my fears were all for nothing.'

Sara drew back as they neared the steps. 'What fears, Mrs. Kyle?'

Helen Kyle paused. 'Jarrod is almost thirty-five. Both J.K. and I want to see him happily married with a family of his own. I was afraid—oh, surely you can understand how it is! I was afraid you might be a different kind of girl, an older girl in experience, if you understand me, one who might try to jeopardise any plans Jarrod might have for marriage.'

Sara felt the familiar twinges of nausea deep in the pit of her stomach, which always occurred when she was deeply disturbed.

'You—you have nothing to fear from me, Mrs. Kyle,' she said tightly.

'No. No, I can see that,' replied Helen Kyle, gripping her arm to assist her to mount the steps. 'I think we might conceivably become friends, which would please J.K. enormously.' She smiled for the first time since Jarrod went into the house. 'You must understand, Sara, I don't mean to be unkind.

It's as well to iron out these difficulties from the very beginning. Then we understand one another. Don't you agree?'

'Oh yes, Mrs. Kyle,' said Sara stiffly. 'We understand one another.'

Her delight in her surroundings, in the luxurious opulence of Flamingo Lodge, had all been doused. When they entered the wide arched entrance which gave on to a cool mosaic-tiled hall, and turned into an exotically furnished lounge where Jarrod and Matt were having drinks, Sara could barely summon up enough energy to show any enthusiasm. Her cheeks were a little pale, and she badly wanted to cry for some inexplicable reason. But instead she had to accept a glass of fresh iced fruit juice, and answer when spoken to, while Jarrod and Matt and Helen chatted quite amicably about London and the family business, and the appalling state of the weather there.

Several times Sara found Jarrod regarding her strangely, as though aware that all was not well with her, and she had to force herself not to allow her eyes to hold his, mirroring her own inner torments as they did.

'I have dined,' Helen was saying now, 'and as you've had such a long journey, I thought you all might prefer supper in your rooms. Sophie has some delicious salad and there's plenty of shellfish to choose from. Which would you prefer, Sara? Crab, lobster, prawns?'

Sara swallowed hard. 'Would—would you consider me very impolite if I said I wanted nothing?' she murmured awkwardly. 'I—I'm not hungry!'

Jarrod frowned now. 'You must be. You haven't

eaten since lunch in New York!'

'I can assure you I'm not,' replied Sara tightly. 'Could—could I go to my room? I—I feel rather tired!'

Helen rang the bell nearby. 'Of course,' she said smoothly, and as the maid Sophie appeared, 'Will you take Miss Robins to her room, Sophie?' She looked at Sara. 'Goodnight then, Sara. I expect we'll meet at breakfast.'

'Yes. Yes, thank you.' Sara nodded her goodnights, and followed Sophie out into the hall again, and up a flight of white-balustraded stairs. The stairs were of the same marble mosaic as the lower hall, and led up to a landing that ran from front to back of the house, with doors opening off both sides, rather like a gallery. Sophie led her to a room at the far end, where the lights from the hall could only faintly be seen, and the bulbs were more discreetly toned. The maid flung open her door, and Sara entered yet another luxurious bedroom. This time the floor was polished wood, strewn with rugs, while the bedspread and curtains were of a brilliant kind of folk weave. The furniture was rather old-fashioned, but highly polished. Beyond was a tiny bathroom, which Sophie said was her own. Her cases had been deposited in the centre of the floor, but were not yet unpacked, and Sara felt too tired to tackle anything of that kind tonight. Instead, she stripped off the slack suit, gave herself a thorough wash, and then put on the shortie cambric nightie which she had worn the previous night in New York.

A lump seemed to have settled itself permanently in her throat, but she was determined she would not give in to tears. Tears were too easy a way out, and were for children, not young women. In ten days she would be eighteen. It was time she started acting like a young woman, instead of a stupid schoolgirl. Letting Helen Kyle's words bother her, that was the most stupid thing of all. After all, what had she said? That Jarrod was soon to marry and settle down; that she didn't want Sara interfering, even unwittingly, in his marriage plans; that some less scrupulous girl might have tried to capitalise on the situation.

She climbed into bed, turning out the main light, but leaving a lamp burning beside the bed. She lifted the paperback she had brought with her from Malthorpe. It was a thriller, and just the sort of reading for someone in her frame of mind, she thought, but even so she found it impossible to concentrate. After reading one page half a dozen times without really understanding it, she gave it up and put her book down. She slid out of bed again, and opened the shutters. Even in the moonless dark she could pick out the lights of other villas lower down the hillside, and smell the delicious tang of the sea. Her room must have a marvellous view, she thought, trying to derive some satisfaction from the thought. But she felt little emotion about that. It came home to her very clearly that circumstances and surroundings were only relative, and that it was people and not things that made or broke one's life.

With that profound thought she padded back to bed, taking another look at her immediate surroundings. She wished she had some cigarettes; she might have tried one, maybe it would have helped her to sleep. As it was she felt much too wide awake and restless. She thought of J.K. alone at Malthorpe, and shivered. If only she was still there! She had fooled herself on Jarrod's plane into believing she could enjoy this holiday. She had been very silly. And two weeks could seem a lifetime. Hadn't she already experienced that when her grandfather died?

There was a sound outside her door, and a light tap, and thinking it was Sophie, she called, 'Come in!' To her astonishment, Jarrod entered the room, closing the door and leaning back against it, regarding her with dark brooding eyes. Sara became again conscious of her attire, as once before, only this time she had not even a housecoat to wrap about her. It was still in her case.

'What do you want?' she exclaimed, and he said softly:

'Don't shout! Unless you want the whole household in here!' He frowned. 'Get into bed!'

Sara hastily scrambled under the bedclothes, drawing them up to her chin, drawing her knees up too, and regarding him over the top rather endearingly. Her hair fell forward, partly covering one cheek, and she brushed it back with a careless hand. 'Well,' she whispered, 'what is it?'

Jarrod straightened, and walked across to the bed, looking down at her. 'What did Helen say to you outside?'

Sara's revealing colour burned in her cheeks. 'Nothing much. Why?'

Jarrod sighed. 'Oh, don't give me that,' he exclaimed, almost raising his voice, until she looked at him in surprise. 'You know damn nicely she said something to upset you, and I want to know what it was! What it was that changed you from a talkative teenager into a tongue-tied waif with no thoughts except escape—from all of us!'

Sara sighed. 'Why don't you ask her?'

'I'm asking you.'

'Well, I can't answer you.' Sara compressed her lips. 'Now, will you please go?'

'Blast you, no! I mean to have an answer!'

'Well, you won't get one from me,' retorted Sara, stiffening her shoulders. 'Go to bed! It's getting late! You must be tired, too.'

Jarrod looked at her irritably. 'I am tired, I admit, very tired, but how the hell am I expected to sleep knowing you're worrying yourself sick over something!'

Sara's lashes veiled her eyes. 'I—I'm not worried,' she said quickly.

'Aren't you? Aren't you just?' Jarrod studied her downbent head and she, becoming aware of his scrutiny, moved uncomfortably.

'Oh lord,' she said, 'why must everyone need to know the far end of everything to do with me? I don't ask a lot of questions! I'm not continually criticising you! Why must you always treat me like an infant?'

Jarrod shrugged his broad shoulders. 'I guess because that's what you are,' he muttered a trifle harshly.

'Am I?' She looked up at him. 'Am I really? Is that all you ever see me as? A dumb kid?'

Jarrod's eyes held hers. 'I didn't say dumb!' he said shortly.

'No, but as good as. I'm eighteen in ten days, Jarrod!'

Her eyes at last fell before his. She was no match for his unblinking gaze, yet she was aware that he was not as indifferent as he would have her believe.

'What do you want me to say, Sara?' he muttered, going down on his haunches beside the bed, forcing her gaze to meet his. 'Is this some new game you're playing? Has your success with the boys from Malthorpe given you a taste for adventure, because I ought to warn you, it's a very dangerous game.'

Sara shivered. 'But you play it,' she said, almost soundlessly.

'With you?' He shook his head. 'No, honey, never that!'

'Why? Am I so repulsive?' Sara was conscious of the depth of the water she was so carelessly entering.

'You're not repulsive at all,' he said huskily, his eyes not mocking or derisive as she had expected, but gentle.

Yet conversely, Sara did not want him to be gentle. She didn't want his pity, his compassion, his understanding of the emptiness inside her.

'Oh, go away,' she said, pressing the knuckles of one hand against her mouth.

'Sara,' he muttered, 'I'm trying to be patient, to understand this urge you have to try out your feminine appeal. Just don't try me too far!'

'Why?' She glared at him. 'Why?' she taunted him again. 'What will you do? What will the gorgeous sexy Jarrod Kyle do?'

Jarrod's eyes were no longer warm and gentle, but angry and glittering, and she felt suddenly excited, in a way she had never experienced before. She knew she ought to feel frightened, afraid of the anger she had aroused in him, afraid of what

137

vengeance he might take. Yet she wasn't. Instead, she realised she wanted nothing more than that he should touch her, that she should feel those hard hands caressing her, and feel that angry, arrogant mouth against her own.

But to her intense disappointment Jarrod got abruptly to his feet, and without speaking walked towards the door. Refusing to let him see how he had disturbed her, she turned her back on him, and she heard the door open very quietly, and close again with a definite click.

Then the whole weight of her actions fell on her, and the tears which had threatened all evening began to fall without hope of quelling them. Not only had she allowed Jarrod to see that she was attracted by him, but he had rejected her, spurned her puny efforts at arousing him. All she had done was make a complete ass of herself, and ruined what might, possibly, have been a good holiday.

What would J.K. think of her if he ever found out? Was Jarrod likely to tell him? J.K. who had thought Jarrod was not to be trusted! How wrong could you be! And Helen! Heavens, she had let everyone down, most of all herself. That night at Malthorpe, when Jarrod had looked at her so disturbingly, she had practically shown then that she was vulnerable. And now, tonight, she had behaved without rhyme or reason. With wanton carelessness! What must Jarrod think of her? He must despise her, utterly!

With a groan, she buried her face in the pillow, trying to obliviate the knowledge that she had lost all her self-respect.

CHAPTER EIGHT

THE next morning Sara woke with an awful feeling of apprehension. At first she couldn't remember why she should feel this way, and then remembrance of the previous evening came flooding back to torment her. Refusing to allow her thoughts to become all-enveloping, she slid out of bed and ran to the window.

The view was as spectacular as she had imagined it to be. The thickly wooded hillside fell away below her window, dotted here and there with the tiled roofs of other dwellings. Colourful trees and shrubs threaded among the foliage, and she wondered what were all their names. There was a beautiful cascade of golden blossom just below in the gardens, and to the right she glimpsed a curved swimming pool edged about with bushes of oleander and rose. A tiled surround sported airbeds and bamboo furniture, upholstered in vivid shades of red and blue and green. It was the most picturesque scene she had ever looked on and even her depression lifted a little on a morning like this. A glance at the small clock on her bedside table told her it was only seven-thirty, but she felt she couldn't stay in bed any longer.

Rummaging through her cases, she brought out a short semi-flared skirt of red crimplene, and donned a sleeveless white sweater to go with it. After a brisk wash in cold water and a hasty run of the comb through her hair she was ready, and she opened her room door quietly in case the rest of the household was still sleeping.

She tiptoed along the landing, and down the stairs to the hall below. Glancing into the lounge which they had entered the previous evening she found it to be deserted, but there was the faint sound of activity to the left of the hall, so she walked across quietly to investigate. She found a small dining-room, but there was no one actually in the room. Instead, french doors stood wide open on to a terrace, with a carved wrought iron rail. A round table was set for breakfast, and Matt was sitting, lazily reading a newspaper as he ate a very English breakfast of bacon, eggs and tomatoes.

Sara ventured into the room tentatively, and Matt, seeing her shadow, said: 'Well, hello, Sara! Coming to join me?'

'Thank you. I'd like to,' Sara nodded, and crossed to the french doors. Then she caught her breath as she ran to the rail and gazed down on the blue waters of the Caribbean, spread out below them. Her room, situated at the side of the house, had merely given her a glimpse of the sea on the horizon, but here the land fell away more steeply, and a sandy basin below them gave on to the creamy surf of the blue water. Palms planted just below the terrace added their own touch of tropicality to the view, and Matt smiled at her enthusiasm.

'Some place to eat a meal, eh?' he remarked, folding his newspaper.

Sara glanced round, her eyes alight with wonder. 'It's like a scene from a film,' she exclaimed. 'How on earth can Jarrod bear to leave all this and return to England!'

She realised as soon as she had spoken that they were not alone, and she turned to face Helen Kyle with some trepidation. Only yesterday she had practically told Jarrod's mother that she addressed him as Mr. Kyle, and now here she was, saying Jarrod as naturally as though she had never used anything else.

'Oh—er—good morning, Mrs. Kyle,' she said awkwardly.

Helen Kyle gave her a slight nod. 'Good morning, Sara. You're an early riser, too, I see.'

'It—it was too nice to stay in bed,' said Sara, somewhat defensively, and then leant against the rail, trying to recapture her excitement at the view.

Helen Kyle seated herself at the table, and when a white-coated manservant appeared, she said: 'What would you like for breakfast, Sara? We have the usual English things, or there's rolls and butter, fruit juice; you choose.'

Sara turned and as Matt held out her chair, sat down too. 'Could I have some fruit juice, and some rolls?' she asked.

'Of course. You heard that, Remus?'

'Yes'm.' Remus beamed and disappeared to get the necessary cutlery. He returned to lay Sara's place, bringing a jug of steaming coffee and some cream. Sara wished Helen had not appeared just then. She could have enjoyed a relaxed meal with only Matt for company. With him she had no inhibitions, and his lazy manner appealed to her.

'What do you plan today, Matt?' Helen was asking now.

Matt shrugged. 'I don't know exactly. Jarrod said something about taking out the yacht. Unless he changes his mind.'

'A yacht!' exclaimed Sara. 'Oh, where is it?'

'There—out in the bay!' Matt raised his arm and pointed, and Sara could see a white hull and some silvery attachments gleaming in the sun 'The *Sea Witch*! Do you sail?'

Sara grimaced. 'Well, it's not exactly common to people like me,' she laughed, relaxing a little.

'Matt's father owns a shipyard,' remarked Helen Kyle conversationally. 'In Norfolk, isn't that so, Matt?'

Matt nodded, and Sara frowned. Somehow she had thought of Matt as being like herself, and to discover that his father owned a shipyard placed him in an entirely different light.

'It was Arnold, Matt's father, who built the *Sea Witch*,' Helen went on. 'Beautiful, isn't she?'

'Yes,' said Sara doubtfully, and caught Matt's eyes upon her.

'What's wrong?' he asked. 'Does it surprise you that unlike Jarrod I'm not following in Father's footsteps?'

Sara shrugged. 'I suppose I didn't think of you as —well, being anything other than—than'—she glanced at Helen—'than Jarrod's assistant.'

Helen seemed to understand this more easily than Matt did. 'Matt prefers the world of high finance to the quiet backwaters of the Broads, even though Arnold gets orders from all over the world, don't you, Matt?' She patted his hand. 'As Jarrod's assistant he is a person in his own right.'

Sara sighed. 'Yes, I suppose so,' she murmured quietly.

'Where is Jarrod, anyway?' asked Helen suddenly.

Matt finished his coffee. 'He went out with Aristotle an hour ago. I believe they were heading for the beach. They took oxygen cylinders with them.'

Sara's eyes were wide. She had thought Jarrod still in bed. To know he was up and about, and likely to appear at any moment, petrified her. However would she face him after last night?

Helen's breakfast consisted of coffee and cigarettes. She seemed to smoke a lot, and maybe that accounted for her slenderness. This morning, in slacks and silk blouse, she did not look a great deal older than Tracy Merrick. They had similar figures and Sara thought they probably got along well together. Tracy would constitute a suitable candidate for the position of Mrs. Jarrod Kyle.

Helen now looked at Sara thoughtfully. 'Perhaps you'd like to take Sara to the beach, Matt,' she suggested, embarrassing Sara by her assumption.

'No—really——' she began, when Matt said:

'I'd like nothing better. I guess you want Jarrod to yourself, is that right?'

Mrs. Kyle smiled. 'You understand me so well, Matt. Of course, I shall adore having some time alone with my son on his return. Where do you plan to go?'

Matt frowned. 'Well, as Jarrod has taken the diving gear, I suggest Sara and I go to Coral Point. The beach is quiet and sheltered by the palms, and the water is pretty shallow.' He glanced at Sara. 'You do swim?'

Sara nodded. 'Yes—but honestly, Matt, it's not necessary. I can amuse myself. After all, the pool here would suit me just as well.'

'Don't be silly, Sara,' said Helen Kyle coolly. 'I insist that you see a little of the place you've chosen for your holiday. Afterwards, Matt may take you in to Kingston for lunch, so be prepared for every eventuality.'

Sara had the feeling that Helen was quietly telling Matt exactly what she wanted him to do, and she felt uncomfortably aware that Jarrod's mother wanted her off the property for some time. After all, the pool was there, and after yesterday's travelling she would have liked to relax in a lounger in the sunshine, or in the shade of one of the beach umbrellas near the lilos in the garden.

Matt seemed unperturbed, however. After she had finished her rolls and coffee, he said: 'Go get your swimsuit, Sara, and we'll be off. Bring some sunglasses if you have them.'

Sara rose obediently to her feet and did as she was bidden. The gates of Flamingo Lodge might stand wide, but there was less freedom of movement here than there was in the confined surroundings of Malthorpe Hall. She felt a pang of homesickness for J.K. and wondered whether she might be able to ring him as Helen had rung Jarrod. After all, he had always told her to use the allowance he made her, but so far she had scarcely touched it. It would be a simple matter to have them reverse the charges, and J.K. wouldn't object. The idea appealed to her; it seemed to bring J.K. and home, for that was what Malthorpe Hall had become, nearer to her.

Collecting her swimsuit, a navy blue and white striped bikini, from her suitcase, she pushed it in a basket bag she had brought with her containing her overnight things, and added a comb, some lip-

144

stick and her sunglasses. She glanced regretfully at her cases, but decided the unpacking of them would have to wait until later.

Matt was waiting for her in the hall. Unlike Jarrod, he was dark, with a stockier appearance although he was almost as tall. Dressed in cream shorts and a pale blue island cotton shirt, he looked cool and attractive, and Sara wondered why the prospect of going out with him didn't arouse more enthusiasm inside her.

Helen came to wish them goodbye, and Sara couldn't help wondering whether her main object was to see them off the property. But such uncharitable thoughts were alien to her and she thrust them impatiently aside.

The cream convertible awaited them, and she wondered what car Jarrod and Aristotle had taken Matt helped her into her seat, and then walked round the bonnet to slide in beside her. He grinned at her as she slid the sunglasses on to her nose. 'Boy, am I lucky!' he remarked laughingly.

'Why?' Sara looked puzzled.

'Well, here I am, being paid for taking out one of the most attractive young women I've ever had the good luck to meet!' he answered.

'Paid?' She frowned.

'Sure. Jarrod insists on paying me during holidays the same as always.'

'Oh, I see.' Sara relaxed. 'You're very polite. Thank you, Matt. But maybe you've been saddled with me!' she grimaced, as they left the gates of Flamingo Lodge behind them.

'Don't be silly.' Now Matt looked solemn. 'Believe me, if I hadn't wanted to bring you, I shouldn't have done so, Helen or no Helen.'

'You realised she was manipulating you?'

'Helen doesn't manipulate me. I'm no puppet,' he answered, swinging round an intersection. 'She thinks she does, that's all. You must learn to listen to Helen, to pretend to act upon her advice and then go your own merry way.'

'Is that what Jarrod does?'

Matt laughed. 'Jarrod? Oh, Sara, you'll learn that Jarrod is a law unto himself. Helen gets nowhere with him. Just as she never succeeded in manipulating J.K. Hasn't he told you they were never compatible?'

'Well yes.'

'And surely you realise that Jarrod is like his father.'

'Yes,' said Sara, more slowly.

'Then that should answer your question. Nevertheless, Helen is very possessive where Jarrod is concerned, so don't be alarmed if she attempts to run your life to her designs. As I say, do what *you* want to do! Jarrod would say the same.'

Sara doubted this, and then sighed. 'It's all so complicated,' she said heavily. 'I wish—I really wish I'd never come.'

'Why?' Matt gave her an astounded look. 'Heavens, don't let Helen get under your skin!'

Sara felt dejected. Matt was a little late in saying that. She had already let Helen get under her skin to the extent of causing the most dreadful rift with Jarrod yet.

Despite her misgivings and anxieties, she found she had a marvellous day with Matt. During the morning they went to the beach Matt had suggested, and Sara had her first taste of bathing in really warm water. Then they lay on the sands, sunbathing, Matt seeming to find Sara's healthy young face and body quite irresistibly good to look at. Curiously, he didn't embarrass her as Jarrod would have done, and she could only assume that kind and gentle though Matt might be she could never see him in the role of a lover. *A lover!* She brought herself up short. Was that how she was imagining Jarrod in her foolishness?

'Tell me,' said Matt, as they sat at lunch in a hotel in the heart of Kingston's bustling main street, 'why were you surprised when Helen told you about my father—and the shipyard?'

Sara shrugged. 'I guess because I'd thought of you as being Jarrod's employee—you know, someone who *had* to work for a living, and instead, you're more his contemporary.'

'Jarrod and I were at Cambridge together,' said Matt thoughtfully. 'He seemed so fired with enthusiasm for the business, for the whole company—his ideas for expansion and so on, that I was fired, too, and the textile trade interested me much more than shipbuilding had ever done. I was interested in design—I fancied myself as a bit of an artist, and Jarrod encouraged me. Eventually, when Jarrod became a cog in the wheel, I joined him, and when he became chairman when his father was taken ill, I became his personal assistant.'

'I see. And doesn't your father mind?'

'Not particularly. I have three brothers and two sisters, all fascinated by messing about in boats, so I won't be missed!'

'Oh!' Sara smiled. 'And do you paint at all now? I mean—design things, and so on?'

'Sometimes, not very successfully, actually. I prefer painting for pleasure now. I usually have an attempt at the view from the terrace where we breakfasted this morning every time I come here.'

Sara was interested. 'Oh, do you? Do you have any paintings I could see? I adore painting myself, and I'd love to see some of your work.'

Matt nodded and grinned. 'Come up and see my etchings,' he intoned in a deep voice, and she laughed merrily.

During the afternoon, he took her on a conducted tour of the city. He showed her the burial place of Admiral Benbow, the official residence of the governor of the island, and the busy harbour bazaar. The stalls fascinated her with their variety and colour, and she had never seen so many different types of fruit, from the banana and orange to the exotic-sounding paw-paw and sapodilla.

It was early evening when they began the ascent into the hills to Flamingo Lodge, and Sara, who had been gay and talkative all day, seemed to withdraw into herself.

'What's troubling you?' asked Matt, frowning. 'You've got me on hand if you need someone to lean on.'

Sara looked at him warmly. 'Have I, Matt? You make me feel much better.'

Matt sighed. 'And you make me feel old.'

'You're not old!'

'I'm thirty-four, twice your age!'

'Only for the moment. I shall be eighteen in nine days' time.'

'Shall you, indeed? We must do something about a party.'

'Oh no!' Sara was horrified. 'Don't tell Mrs. Kyle, please. I want no fuss!'

'Oh, all right, Sara, but stop behaving so nervously. There's absolutely nothing to be nervous about.'

The lights of the villa gleamed as they had the night before, but tonight Sara felt no pleasure at the sight. Instead she felt an awful feeling of apprehension that was heightened when they halted at the front verandah, and Jarrod came to stand at the top of the steps, regarding them broodingly.

'Where the hell have you been?' he said, as they got out, Sara gathering together her belongings and thrusting them into her bag.

'You know where we've been,' replied Matt calmly. 'Helen must have told you we went to Coral Point.'

Jarrod frowned. Dressed in dark pants and a dark shirt, he looked very attractive, and Sara felt her heart somersault uncomfortably inside her.

'You went to Coral Point ten hours ago. I drove there myself around lunchtime. You were not there then!'

Matt raised his eyebrows. 'Now why should you do a thing like that?' he asked lazily, taking Sara's arm and assisting her up the shallow steps. 'We went in to Kingston for lunch, and afterwards we did some sightseeing.' He glanced at Sara. 'Helen knew we were not expected back.'

Jarrod chewed at the cigar between his teeth. 'I don't give a damn what Helen knew,' he swore angrily.

'Now cool it,' said Matt, without turning a hair. 'We're here, aren't we? All safe and sound! And we've had a marvellous day, haven't we, Sara?'

Sara nodded, not trusting herself to speak as Jarrod's gaze flickered over her, lingering momentarily on the shortness of her skirt.

'Well, it's seven-thirty,' he said tautly. 'Dinner is at eight this evening. Helen has invited the McKays over. I suggest you both go and get changed!'

'Sure thing,' agreed Matt, seeming a trifle amused by Jarrod's attitude. 'Come on, Sara!'

Sara did not linger, hastening ahead of Matt up the stairs. 'Don't rush,' he said lazily, behind her. 'Jarrod's good and mad! Give him time to cool off!'

'But why? I mean, why is he mad?' Sara's head was spinning.

'I guess he takes his role as your guardian rather seriously, honey. And so he should. You're far too attractive to be left to run around loose for every guy to try and get fresh with. Maybe he sees himself as a father figure!'

Sara pressed a hand to her throat. 'I see,' she murmured chokily. 'See—see you later, Matt. And thank you for a wonderful day!'

'Thank *you*!' returned Matt, with a cheerful grin, and disappeared into his room.

In Sara's room, her cases had been unpacked for her, and her clothes ironed and hung in her wardrobe. There was nothing for her to do but bathe and change, and so she went through to her bathroom and turned on the bath taps. Then she went back into her room and studied the door for a moment. A key was inserted into the lock, and she frowned. She was sure that had not been there before. Had someone placed it there? But who? Not Jarrod. He had no reason to suppose she would lock him out.

Nevertheless, as the key was there, she walked across and turned it before re-entering the bathroom. Afterwards, she studied her clothes with some concentration. She wanted something attractive to wear, something young and yet not girlish. Eventually she chose a midnight blue lurex-threaded silk, with a tunic-type skirt that fell from a slender band of pearls just below her breasts. The short skirt was edged with pearls, and there was a pearl-edged scoop neckline. It was sleeveless, and the slight tan she had acquired that day added to her appearance.

The McKays had arrived when she descended the stairs to find everyone talking together in the long lounge. There was Helen and Matt, and Jarrod of course, and two other couples; Frank and Lorna McKay, who were Helen's age, and a young man and woman who were the McKays' son and daughter, Mark and Virginia. Helen performed the introductions while Jarrod mixed drinks at the bar in the corner. They all seemed to be drinking long drinks which Matt told her were daiquiris, but Jarrod handed her an innocuous-looking lime liquid remarking:

'Fresh lime and lemon, laced with the smallest part of vodka. I think you'll like it.'

'Thank you.' Sara took the drink and Jarrod nodded and turned away without looking at her. She sighed. How cold and polite he was tonight. What was he thinking, under that icy exterior? Had he noticed her at all? Did he like her dress? Or was she just part of the decoration?

Virginia McKay was yet another girl to find Jarrod attractive. Sara thought it was inevitable perhaps, as Lorna McKay and Helen Kyle seemed such good friends. Mark McKay was a pale, ineffectual youth, older than Sara, but callow in her opinion, and she didn't encourage him when he tried to have a conversation with her. After Matt, and Jarrod of course, Mark was very dull company. Maybe because all her life she had been in the company of older men she found boys of her own age boring, but somehow she could never see herself becoming interested in someone with so little vigour or vitality.

Dinner was served in a small dining-room at a polished rosewood table that was set with lace place mats and crystal glass goblets. Sara ate very little, even the spiced delicacy of roast sucking pig not arousing much appetite inside her. Though Jarrod did not speak to her, she was conscious of him and his displeasure the whole evening, and when the meal was over she escaped on to the terrace with some relief.

Matt was being employed by Helen to roll back the carpet in the lounge for dancing, and Virginia McKay was sorting through some records and messing about with a tape recorder with Jarrod. When the music came through to her it was low and rhythmic, a steel band playing some of the exciting limbo music of the islands. She could hear laughter and talk from within, but had no desire to join them. Out here, on the terrace, looking down on the lights below and smelling the fragrant perfume of the night air, she attempted to achieve some kind of detachment.

A sound behind her startled her. She had not bothered to turn on the lights in the morning-room behind her, and she had thought no one knew where she was. But her silhouette gave her away, and she drew back as a dark shadow detached itself from the gloom and joined her on the terrace. She knew at once that it was Jarrod. His silvery blond hair gleamed in the pale light and even as she watched he flicked a switch that lit a lamp on the small curvature of the terrace.

Sara gripped the rail with taut fingers, willing herself not to turn towards him.

'Well?' he said softly. 'I gather you found Matt good company.'

'Shouldn't I?' she parried uncomfortably.

'I don't know. What did he do?' Jarrod's voice was still angry.

'What do you mean, what did he do? He didn't *do* anything. We just bathed, and sunbathed, and then had lunch, like he said. I didn't know I would have to give an account of myself, or I would have taken a notebook!'

'Don't taunt me, Sara,' he muttered savagely. 'I've decided to ignore your little seduction scene last night, but I will not have you behaving like some— some—young idiot! For heaven's sake, Sara, as you said, you're almost eighteen. Old enough to know that men can be dangerous, with sufficient provocation.'

Sara sighed. 'Oh, please,' she exclaimed, 'don't let's start that all over again.'

'All right, all right. I have no intention of starting anything. I just want you to know that you needn't go around feeling afraid of me. I'm sorry if unwittingly I've aroused your resentment, but I've decided that we don't know one another well enough, and that's why you're acting this way. I suppose it's understandable, really. I am your guardian after all, and I've shown little or no interest in you to date. In your character, that is—your personality! I intend to remedy that, starting tomorrow.'

Sara felt her heartbeats quicken. 'That—that's not necessary!'

'Oh, but it is. So, tomorrow, we'll begin by teaching you to swim underwater, and then maybe a little water-skiing. I know you'll enjoy that.' He was controlling his temper quite easily now. 'You agree?'

Sara sighed. 'Do I have any choice?'

'Sara,' he muttered warningly.

'Oh—oh, all right, Mr. Kyle. I'll fall in with your plans. Just don't expect me to fall over myself to please you like all the others do!'

Her remarks were stupid, and childish, and with a muffled exclamation he turned and walked across the morning-room to the doorway into the hall. Then he turned.

'I shall expect you to be ready to leave at eight-thirty in the morning,' he said shortly, and without waiting for her reply, he left her.

CHAPTER NINE

In spite of Sara's dismay at Jarrod's intentions, she found during the next few days that Jarrod could be the most charming and amusing of companions. Disregarding his mother's pleas that he should spend more time with her, visit the McKays, play a little golf, he persisted in taking Sara everywhere with him. Matt joined them occasionally, but much to Sara's surprise Jarrod found his personal assistant tasks to perform during the long lazy days, leaving Sara to face hours alone with himself.

Not that the hours passed slowly. Together with Aristotle, he had taught her how to swim underwater, and although she had not ventured very far into deep water, she had glimpsed a little of the wonder of the world beneath the calm surface. She had seen exquisite rock formations, stumbled upon sleeping starfish and crustaceans, and fingered the sharp yet delicate filigree of the coral strands. Aristotle was never far away from her side, acting like the bodyguard Jarrod had at first said he was, making her laugh with his solemn admonitions which he delivered with a gleaming smile.

Another day they had taken the motor boat to a deep bay where a jetty had been erected to give elevation for would-be water-skirs. Sara, who had found the underwater swimming quite easy to master, found water-skiing a much different proposition, and sank ignominiously into the waves so many times that she eventually had to give it up, her legs ached so much.

And all the while she was conscious of Jarrod; conscious of his lean brown body, seldom clad in more than swimming shorts and light wool sweater, conscious of the vitality that emanated from him, whose magnetism enveloped her, conscious of the times when he was explaining something to her and she would turn to find his eyes regarding her strangely, almost as though he hated her. She couldn't understand why he should look at her in this way, unless her previous actions had condemned her in his eyes, made him despise her. And yet, if this were so, why did he take the trouble to spend so much time with her, entertaining her, preventing her from becoming involved with Matt, or anyone else for that matter? It didn't make sense, and Sara gave it up as being completely incomprehensible.

But despite this veiled antagonism, there were times, times when she thought he forgot who she was, when he made her laugh and laughed with her, teasing her, interesting her in the antics of a sand crab, lying beside her in the sand, and telling her about his life, the countries he had visited, and the things he had done just for kicks. Those were the times Sara liked best, and she stored them up inside her, aware that her feelings for him were becoming irretrievable somehow. There was no doubt in her mind any longer, and the knowledge that her emotions no longer obeyed the dictates of her mind frightened her a little.

One afternoon he took her out on the *Sea Witch*, with Aristotle to act as crew. The swing and sway of the craft was alarming at first, and Sara clung to the side, praying that they would not capsize, trying to prevent the nausea rising inside her. But after a while she became used to it, and relaxed, and as her nerves disappeared, so did the nausea. Jarrod seemed pleased that she was a good sailor, and she was quite pleased herself.

In the evenings, Helen invariably had company for dinner, or arrangements had been made for herself and Jarrod to dine out. Sometimes Jarrod refused to go out, and stayed home and played gin rummy with Matt and Sara, but at others he accompanied his mother, leaving Matt and Sara alone with some obvious misgivings.

Matt seemed amused at Jarrod's annoyance at these times, and said: 'Your guardian seems to be taking his duties very seriously these days. Don't you think so?'

Sara shrugged, colouring as usual. 'I don't know why you should think that,' she murmured, studying the cards in her hand.

'Don't you?' Matt cupped his chin on his hand, 'Sure you do, Sara. You're perfectly aware why I should think that. Jarrod hasn't left you alone since our first day here. He spends all day and every day in your company. Now that's not usual, is it?'

Sara sighed. 'Oh, I don't know. Must we discuss it?'

'Yes, I think we must. I used to think I knew Jarrod pretty well. Now I've realised I don't know him at all.'

'But why?' Sara's eyes were puzzled.

'Man, surely you can see that for Jarrod to spend so much time with you and ignore the usual pursuits of the rich young tycoon in the West Indies is quite something! Hell, Helen is practically gnawing off the ends of her fingers! She finished off her nails some time ago!'

Sara couldn't suppress a smile. 'You're exaggerating!'

'Maybe I am. But that doesn't alter the fact that you are receiving the full treatment.'

'What on earth do you mean?' Sara laid down her cards.

Matt sniffed. 'Aw, come on, let's get on with the game!'

She shook her head. 'No. You started this, now tell me, what do you mean?'

'Well, I guess if I didn't know Jarrod better, I'd say that he was becoming—hell, is!' he corrected himself, '—interested in you!'

Sara put her hands on her knees so that he should not see that they were trembling. 'Matt! Don't be so ridiculous!'

Matt sighed. 'Yes, I know, I know. It sounds ridiculous to me, too, and yet—well, that's how it looks!'

Sara rose jerkily to her feet. 'Well, you couldn't be more wrong!' she exclaimed.

'Why?' Matt lay back in his chair. 'Now, you tell me why?'

'Well, for a start, Jarrod doesn't see me as—as—as a woman, only as a child, a kid—a nuisance, mainly!'

'Are you sure?'

Sara bit hard at her lip. 'Oh, yes, I'm sure,' she murmured bitterly.

Matt shook his head. 'Ah, well, so be it! But take

it easy, Sara; oh, I know that's rich, coming from me, but—well, I've known Jarrod a long time.'

Sara sat down again, to prevent her legs from giving out on her. 'Sh—shall we get on with the game?' she asked, picking up her cards.

Matt gave her a wry glance, and then nodded.

Sara's birthday dawned bright and clear. She was growing used to these wonderful mornings, with the air, soft and sweet-smelling, drifting in through the open casements. Her clock told her it was eight-fifteen. She had overslept. She was supposed to be going swimming with Jarrod and Aristotle, to have another lesson in skin-diving. Only Matt knew that it was her birthday, and she had insisted he did not tell anyone else. So the plans for the day had been made as any other day had been.

Sophie, the maid, arrived as she was dressing, in slim-fitting cream pants and a pale blue overblouse. She was carrying a tray on which reposed a jug of fruit juice, a jug of coffee, some hot rolls and curls of butter, and a small pile of envelopes.

Sara's eyes widened in surprise, as Sophie said: 'Happy birthday, Miss Sara!'

'Why, thank you,' she said, smiling. 'Are Mr. Jarrod and Aristotle waiting for me?'

'No, miss. Mr. Jarrod still in bed this morning, and Aristotle, he out in Kingston, shopping for Mrs. Kyle.'

'Oh!' Sara frowned.

'Mr. Jarrod sick,' continued Sophie conversationally.

'Sick?' Sara stared at her. 'Wh—what's wrong with him?'

159

'I'm not sure, miss. Maybe just bad headache, yes?'

Sara nodded, thanked her and after she had gone picked up the envelopes, all addressed to herself. One was from England, and she tore this open first, looking tenderly at the card it contained. Of course it was from J.K., and his greeting brought back all her affection for him. She had never rung him, as she had intended to do, so perhaps she would do it today.

The other cards were from Mrs. Kyle, Matt, the McKays and Jarrod. Jarrod's was plain, and the words he had written the very minimum, merely: *Regards, Jarrod.* Sara sighed, and then stood them up on her dressing table, delighting in the small array they made.

Then she ate her breakfast, and went downstairs with the tray. Sophie was in the hall, and took the tray away from her, and she entered the morning-room, where Matt was sitting breakfasting on the terrace as usual.

'Many happy returns,' he remarked, smiling. 'You look bright and cheerful this morning!'

'Thank you. And thank you for your card. But you really ought not to have told anyone.'

'Who me? I didn't tell anyone.' Matt shook his head. 'I expect your—er—guardian already knew.'

'Oh!' Sara bent her head. 'What's wrong with Jarrod anyway?'

Matt shrugged. 'I suppose he drank a little too much, last night.'

'Oh!' Sara said again.

Matt sighed. 'Hell, I can't tease you now, can I? No, Jarrod has a bad cold, that's all. A chill. Knowing him he'll be up after lunch. But he looked pretty rotten when I saw him an hour ago.'

Sara relaxed. 'I see.' She walked to the rail, looking down on the fabulous view. 'It's a wonderful day.'

'Hmn. It's a shame to spend your birthday tied to the house. How about allowing me to take you into Kingston and buy you some lunch? Then we could spend an hour on the beach, sunbathing.'

Sara glanced at him. 'Don't you have work to do?'

Matt grinned. 'Well, as my lord and master is ill, he hasn't issued any instructions. I'm free as air. And after all, you've achieved womanhood today, haven't you, and it would be a shame to waste it.'

Sara laughed, and leaned back against the rail. 'All right. Why not?' she agreed, nodding. 'As you say, it's a shame to stay at home on my birthday.'

Helen Kyle came into the morning-room soon afterwards, as Matt was finishing his breakfast. 'Oh, good morning, Sara,' she said, rather coolly. Her attitude to Sara was never particularly friendly. 'Happy birthday!'

'Thank you,' Sara smiled.

Helen seated herself at the table. 'I suppose you know Jarrod is ill?' she asked generally.

Sara glanced at Matt, and he said: 'Yes, we do. A chill, isn't it?'

'A severe chill. I suspect he got soaked that day he took out the *Sea Witch*. He never takes any interest in his own wellbeing!'

'Jarrod isn't the kind of man to care whether he caught a chill or not,' remarked Matt dryly. 'And spending so much time in the cold concrete world of the boardroom, he takes every opportunity he can to be out in the fresh air. You wouldn't deny him that, would you, Helen?'

Helen lifted her shoulders eloquently. 'Well, anyway,' she continued, 'he won't be able to entertain you today, Sara, despite the fact that it's your birthday. It's such a shame.' She looked at Matt. 'Aren't you going to offer to be Sara's escort, Matt?'

Matt pushed back his chair. 'I already have,' he returned smoothly. 'We're lunching in Kingston, if you don't mind.'

Helen looked smugly delighted. 'I don't mind at all, Matt,' she replied calmly. 'I'm very pleased that Sara won't have to spend so auspicious a day here, with only myself for company.'

Sara reserved judgement. She was quite aware of Helen's motives for manoeuvring them out of the way. It would give her some time alone with her precious son.

'Well, come along, Sara,' said Matt, now. 'Collect your things. See you later, Helen.'

But somehow the day out was not a success. Previously, Sara had relaxed in Matt's company, but now she couldn't. Whether an undiluted diet of Jarrod's company had spoiled her for anybody else she didn't know, but certainly she found Matt dull company today.

In the afternoon, after more sightseeing, they found a quiet beach, and she lay on her back, eyes closed, sunbathing, while Matt propped himself up on his elbow, looking down at her, studying her at close quarters.

'What do you plan to do with your life?' he murmured, touching the tip of her nose with his finger.

Sara's eyes flickered open. 'Oh, I don't know,' she said uncomfortably, not particularly liking this close scrutiny. 'Why?'

'I never got around to showing you my etchings,' he murmured. 'Jarrod's taken up so much of your time, I never seem to get a look in!' He laughed softly. 'Except today, and I'm enjoying this very much.'

Sara rolled on to her side away from him, looking out to sea with unseeing eyes.

'Say, Sara,' Matt rolled her on to her back again, 'don't turn away. I want to talk to you. Has—has any man ever kissed you, honey?'

Sara sat bolt upright. 'Matt, for heaven's sake!' she exclaimed.

Matt sat up as well. 'What's wrong? This is your birthday, isn't it? I just thought I'd make it a memorable one.'

Sara frowned in amazement. 'How? By kissing me? You've got some conceit!'

'Oh, Sara, stop getting so uppity!' Matt chewed his lip. 'I thought we were friends!'

'Well, so we are. But not kissing kin, so don't get any ideas!' She glanced at her watch. 'It's after four. Don't you think we ought to be getting back?'

Matt grimaced. 'Here,' he said gruffly, handing her a small parcel. 'I had a present for you.'

Sara sighed. 'Oh, Matt, I wish you hadn't.'

'Don't say that, you haven't opened it yet.'

She unwrapped the small box, and opened it to find a pair of jade earrings lying on cotton wool. They were small and delicate, and she felt contrite.

'Oh, Matt!'

'Do you like them?'

163

'Of course I do. But I wish you hadn't spent your money. I'm not worth it.'

Matt shook his head, and got to his feet. 'I wouldn't say that, Sara. Come on, we'll go back.'

Flamingo Lodge seemed deserted when they arrived back. The sun was sinking low and a golden glow tinged every gleaming window pane. Matt brought the car to a halt, and said:

'No welcoming committee! Good!'

Sara frowned. 'I expect Mrs. Kyle is indoors, and Jarrod is most probably still in bed, wouldn't you think?'

Matt shook his head. 'I'd say that was highly unlikely,' he remarked, 'particularly if he's found out that we're out together.'

Sara grimaced. 'Oh well, it is my birthday. Anyway, I'm going to try and ring J.K., to thank him for his card, and to see how he is.' She ran lightly up the steps, and then turned: 'Thanks for taking me out, Matt.'

Matt came up the steps to join her. 'You're welcome, and you know it.' He touched her cheek gently with an affectionate gesture. 'I'm the one who should be thanking you.'

She half-smiled, afraid he was about to say something more, when the mesh door from the hall swung open, and Jarrod stood there, leaning against the jamb, supporting himself with his other hand against the opposite side of the doorway.

'Well!' he said harshly. 'This is a touching scene!'

'Now, Jarrod,' began Matt, but Jarrod merely ignored him.

'Where have you been?' he asked. 'I thought I gave you the Latimer account yesterday, Matt. Have you dealt with it?'

Matt moved uncomfortably now. 'Hell, Jarrod, must we have this inquisition every time we get home? Today—as you seem to have forgotten—is Sara's eighteenth birthday. Some birthday, stuck at home here with no one to talk with—no one to swim with!'

'I'm perfectly aware of the day,' returned Jarrod, straightening.

There was a sound behind him, and Helen emerged, brushing past Jarrod smilingly. 'Oh, you're back,' she said, with affected surprise. 'Have you had a good time?'

'Great!' said Matt, with some sarcasm, feeling in his pockets for his cigarettes. 'Have you?'

Helen frowned. 'Well, of course, I've been busy. We're having a small dinner party this evening—in honour of Sara's birthday, naturally.'

Jarrod glanced her way. 'Whose idea was this?'

'Mine, of course.'

'Then forget it.' Jarrod looked moodily anoyed. 'I have my own plans for this evening, and they don't include a family dinner party!'

Helen stared at him, and Sara felt the palms of her hands grow moist. 'What do you mean, Jarrod?' Helen exclaimed. 'What plans?'

Jarrod thrust his hands into the pockets of his trousers. '*I* am taking Sara out for dinner,' and as his mother would have protested, he continued: 'Every evening you've successfully filled for me, mostly to the exclusion of my ward. This evening, as it's Sara's birthday, I intend to take her out—

alone!'

Helen looked furious. 'You're not fit to go out, Jarrod! You must be running a temperature! I told you to stay in bed this morning!'

Jarrod's jaw tightened, and Sara could have told Helen exactly what that meant. 'My dear Helen,' he said coldly, 'no one—but no one—tells me what to do! I'm not ill—I have a cold, that's all! If I'd been in England, I doubt whether I would have noticed it. As it is you attempt to suffocate me with kindness! You should know by now that that kind of treatment doesn't work with me!'

Helen compressed her thin lips. 'And what about Sara? Have you thought about her feelings? She may not want to go out with you when I've invited several *young* people for dinner!'

Jarrod glanced at Sara. 'Well?' he said bleakly. 'You decide! Do you want to come with me—or stay here and have your party!' His tone was mocking, and Sara disliked his attitude.

Matt intervened. 'You can't ask her a question like that, Jarrod,' he exclaimed. 'As your mother has gone to the trouble——'

'Shut up, Matt!' Jarrod's tone was icy, and Matt shrugged and walked into the house.

Sara moved awkwardly. Now the onus was on her. She wanted to refuse him. She wanted to be scathing, and tell him she would prefer the dinner party Helen had prepared. But the temptation to spend a whole evening in his company was too great, and she dared not look at Helen when she said:

'I—I would like to go out with you, Jarrod.'

Jarrod looked triumphant, and as soon as she had agreed, Sara felt contrite, particularly as Helen was giving her a very spiteful stare.

'So?' said Helen angrily. 'Very well, Jarrod. But don't blame me if you catch pneumonia!' and she turned and marched into the house.

Ignoring her, Jarrod glanced at his watch. 'It's almost six,' he said, looking at Sara with lazy eyes. 'Go and get ready. We're leaving in half an hour.'

Sara did not reply, but merely brushed past him on her way indoors. Again she felt she had let herself down. Again she had allowed him to dictate her life emotionally.

Nevertheless, as she got ready, she couldn't deny the surge of excitement the prospect of the evening ahead aroused in her. She took some time choosing what to wear, and finally decided on a silvery blue chiffon, sleeveless, with a skirt that swirled about her thighs in enchanting swathes. With her hair hanging silkily to her shoulders, she was ready, a white scarf of silk over her arm, in case the evening was cool.

When she reached the hall, Jarrod was already there, tall and attractive in a dark lounge suit and white shirt. He was smoking a cheroot, his eyes appraising as he watched her descend the staircase. Helen appeared from the direction of the kitchen. She was wearing a quilted green housecoat, and gave Sara a malevolent glance.

'So you're really going,' she said, looking at her son.

Jarrod nodded. 'I don't say things I don't mean, you ought to know that by now,' he remarked casually. 'Come along, Sara. See you later, Helen.'

Conscious of Helen's eyes upon her, Sara preceded him out of the door and down the steps to where a dark green open sports car awaited them. He helped her in, and then walked round to slide in beside her. The engine roared to life, and he switched on the radio as they turned out of the drive on to the road.

The wind ruffled their hair, but it was so soft and velvety that Sara didn't mind. She felt exhilarated and frightened, all at the same time, and was determined to enjoy herself, no matter what.

Jarrod didn't speak much on the journey, merely asking her if she was warm enough and whether she wanted a scarf for her hair. They followed the road towards Kingston, but turned inland, through thickly forested areas where the heavy ebony and mahogany trees crowded their path, hiding the smoky light of the pale moon that was rising. Sara wondered where he was taking her. These were roads she had never traversed before, and she gasped at the beauty of the view from this vantage point, the moon gilding the sea, and making swanlike grace of the sloops on its surface, dipping their heads in the gentle breeze.

Then the road curved down again, until neon-lighting signified the object of their travels, a low building, strung with multi-coloured lights, highlighting the words 'Pedro's Marine'. There were plenty of cars parked on the forecourt, and when Jarrod helped her from the car and escorted her across a wide verandah, under an arched entrance and into a brightly lit bar throbbing with the music of a steel band, Sara saw why it possessed so peculiar a name. The bar was situated round a deep sea-water aquarium, in the depths of which was every kind of fish imaginable. Green lighting enhanced its marine appearance, and Sara leaned on the rail in excitement, fascinated by the variety of shapes and colours.

Jarrod came to lean beside her, handing her a tall glass of amber-coloured liquid. 'Here,' he said, 'a small tribute to your maturity. It's rum and ginger ale. Quite an innocuous proportion of rum, believe me!'

Sara found herself smiling, and sipped the drink tentatively. 'Hmn. It's delicious! What are you drinking?'

'Rum and soda. Rather more stimulating, but perfectly safe, I can assure you. Now, what are you going to choose to eat?'

Sara's eyes widened. 'How do you mean?'

'The fish! Surely you realised you chose your meal.'

'No! Do you? Oh—well, I don't know. What do you suggest?'

Jarrod looked down into the well. 'How about baked crab? Have you ever tried that? Or turtle steak?'

Sara gasped, 'Turtle steak! There are no turtles in here.'

'No, but you might enjoy it. With rice perhaps.'

'It sounds interesting,' she admitted. 'Do you recommend it?'

'I recommend anything at Pedro's,' replied Jarrod, as a small dapper little man came to join them. 'Hello, Pedro! How are you?'

'Ah, Señor Kyle!' Pedro grinned happily. 'It is happy I am to see you again. I did not know you were returning here so soon.' He looked at Sara. 'And your companion also. I have not had the pleasure . . . '

Jarrod glanced wryly at Sara. 'Sara, this is Pedro Armendez, proprietor of this establishment. Pedro, meet Sara Robins, my ward.'

If Pedro was surprised at this revelation, he did not show it. Instead, he bowed politely and suggested that Sara have a second drink on the house. Sara politely declined, and after more conversation, Jarrod was shown his table. The restaurant was in an inner apartment, hung about with palms and tropical flowers, and lighted far more discreetly than the bar. A small band played on a corner dais, and several couples revolved on a handkerchief-sized dance floor.

The meal was delicious. After a special kind of soup which Pedro recommended himself, she had turtle steak and fluffy white rice, and finished off with a dessert made of oranges and the pulpy flesh of the star-apple. The coffee was Continental and rich, and Jarrod had a liqueur, although Sara refused, deciding the rum she had already consumed accounted for the feeling of well-being that was flooding her body. She refused to think about Helen, and the possible outcome of this defiance, and concentrated on the moment only.

Jarrod was quite an interesting companion now, telling her about the earthquake at Spanish Town and the overthrow of the despotism in the islands. 'The original name for Jamaica was *Xaymaca*,' he said, sipping his liqueur lazily.

'I didn't know that,' said Sara interestedly. 'What does that mean?'

'The Indian meaning was land of wood and

water,' he replied, 'and I guess that's really what it is.'

'And so marvellously laid out,' enthused Sara, sighing. 'I mean, a land of wood and water could describe practically anywhere, whereas here everything is so much larger than life somehow. The seas are bluer, the trees are greener and flowers are more colourful!' She sighed again.

'You ought to work in our public relations department,' he said, laughing. 'If you could describe textiles with as much enthusiasm as you expend on describing the island, I should imagine you could sell practically anything.'

Sara cupped her face with her hands, resting her elbows on the table 'I'm glad you brought me out, Jarrod.'

'Why?' His eyes narrowed.

'Oh, don't be alarmed, I'm not going to be stupid. It's just that—well, I'm enjoying myself.'

'Good.' Jarrod finished his liqueur, and summoned the waiter. He signed the bill, then said: 'Come on, let's go!'

'Go?' Sara stared at him. 'But it's early yet.'

'I know it. Come on, collect your wrap.'

Sara felt dejected, wishing she had said nothing now. If her words had precipitated their return to Flamingo Lodge she was furious with herself.

She got into the car with ill grace, not glancing at him as he joined her, turning the key in the ignition. Apart from a slight huskiness in his voice, his cold didn't seem to be troubling him at all, so there was absolutely no reason why they should go home so early. It was barely ten.

The car followed the winding road through the

hills, dropping down steeply into the valleys and cresting the small rises without difficulty. It was only as they drove that Sara became aware that they were not going straight back to Helen Kyle's home, for the car was winding lower down the terraces, and soon they were almost to sea-level. The car swung along a headland, and he brought it to a halt above the beach that was silvered with moonlight. Out in the bay, Sara could see a yacht, and she realised it was the *Sea Witch*.

'Don't be alarmed,' remarked Jarrod, 'I'm not aiming to take you sailing. Let's walk on the sand. It's wonderful down here, and we can talk.'

'Talk?' Sara frowned. 'What about?'

Jarrod ignored her, sliding out of the car, so that she was forced to do likewise. The path to the beach was steep, and she took off her shoes, and ran down the slope to the sand. Beyond a belt of palms the sea creamed unceasingly, and the sound of it was in their ears, combined with the faint persistent throbbing of a drumbeat rhythm from one of the villas high up on the terraces. It was a perfect night, and Sara thought she had had almost a perfect birthday.

She ran away from Jarrod to the water's edge, allowing the waves to touch her toes. Jarrod came to join her, hands in his pockets, looking solemn.

'Now,' he said, frowning, 'we can talk.'

'What about?' She sighed. 'Must we talk seriously tonight?'

'Well, I think it's time we considered your future seriously. It's three months and more since you came to live with J.K., and while I know he has no desire to lose you, nevertheless you ought to be thinking about your future.'

Sara felt a cold hand round her heart. 'In what way?' she asked.

'Sara, you must realise that you have to have a career. J.K. doesn't seem to understand that young girls nowadays need something more to occupy themselves with than merely playing around. I think you understand this, and that's why I'm discussing it with you, rather than with him.'

Sara heaved a sigh. 'I see.'

'Here in the islands you've seen a little of the world you had hitherto not known existed. You must have some feelings about it, something of it must have taught you that life has many different faces.'

She nodded. 'I suppose so. Travel broadens the mind, as they say.'

Jarrod thrust his hands into his trouser pockets. 'Matt tells me that you like painting—that you're interested in that sort of career.'

'Sometimes I think I am,' she shrugged.

'I could give you a design career with one of the textile corporations,' he remarked thoughtfully.

She looked at him. 'But not your organisation, I gather.'

He stared out to sea. 'No, not mine,' he agreed.

Sara sighed again. Whenever she seemed to be getting anywhere with Jarrod she seemed to come up against a brick wall.

'Well, I don't want to talk about it now,' she murmured bleakly. 'I might have known that you wouldn't have anything other than business on your mind!'

Jarrod's expression hardened. 'What the hell do you mean?' he swore angrily. 'Haven't I brought you out this evening?'

'Yes, but now I'm beginning to think you had different motives from the ones I imagined.' She compressed her lips mutinously. 'J.K. was right. All you think about is business! I pity the woman who marries you! She'd be falling in love with a machine!'

Jarrod caught her wrist in a painful hold. 'I've warned you, Sara,' he muttered angrily. 'Don't attempt to meddle in things that you don't understand.'

Sara struggled to free herself. 'You continually say that!' she seethed. 'But I understand very well. I understand that Lauren Maxwell, Tracy Merrick, even Virginia McKay, are of little importance to you. You only require a woman from time to time, to satisfy your manly appetites, not someone to share your life, to talk with you, to *love* you! I've just realised how right your father can be! Except in one thing! He thought I'd enjoy this holiday, but instead I'm hating it, do you hear, I'm hating it!'

And with a sob she broke away from him, running blindly up the beach to the belt of trees, her breath coming chokingly, tears obliterating her view so that she stumbled over an old log and fell among the palms, her dress ripping slightly on the branches. She heard him behind her, and rolled on to her back as he halted beside her. His coat was loosened, his hair ruffled, and he looked angrier than she had ever seen him. He stared down at her for a moment, and then flung himself beside her, uncaring of the damp sand against the immaculate dark suit. Sara tried to roll away from him, but he imprisoned her, one hand on either side of her body.

'So,' he muttered savagely, 'you think I'm a machine! God, don't you know how much I've wanted you, Sara!' and his mouth sought and found hers.

At first she struggled, trying to press him away from her, but the weight of his body was too heavy, and after a while the feel of that hard muscular frame against hers seduced her to a state of inertia that drugged her with sensuality.

'Jarrod,' she moaned, 'please!'

He buried his face in her hair. 'I warned you,' he muttered violently, 'but you continued to taunt me. Tonight, in this dress, you're like a witch!' His mouth sought hers again, his kisses slowing and lengthening, arousing her to an awareness of the dangers of this kind of lovemaking. She didn't want to struggle any more, she wanted to wind her arms round his neck, and make him possess her completely.

His hands slid the length of her body, caressing her expertly, while his mouth continued to devour hers, finding too the soft nape of her neck, the creamy curve of her breast, the tanned peach of her cheeks.

She was on fire for him, unable to think coherently, conscious of nothing but the sea and the sand, and Jarrod.

And then, with a positive groan of self-disgust, Jarrod suddenly thrust her away from him, getting to his feet and pushing back his hair with unsteady hands. Sara closed her eyes, momentarily, shutting out the world for a few minutes more. Then she sat up, clenching her fists into tight balls.

'Get up, Sara!' he muttered, turning away. 'Let's

go. Before I lose my head completely.'

She struggled to her feet. 'Jarrod——' she began uncertainly.

He glanced back at her. 'Don't speak to me,' he ground out the words. 'I—I'm sorry for what just occurred. I know that's indequate, but there's nothing more I can say, short of promising to hang myself,' and he turned and strode way through the trees. She followed more slowly. She felt sick and shaken, and she slid into the seat of the car, her legs trembling violently. The engine roared to life, and Jarrod drove away, turning up into the hills towards Flamingo Lodge.

Sara sat in her corner, unable to think coherently. All that kept flooding her brain was Jarrod's rejection of her, and its implications.

At last he said: 'I apologise, of course. It's no part of my duties to give you a sexual education. I disgust myself. I'm sorry.'

Sara stared at him in the gloom. 'It was my fault,' she said, in a small voice. 'You know it was!'

'Nevertheless, I'm old enough to have more sense,' he muttered. 'After the inquisition I gave Matt . . .' His voice trailed away.

'What inquisition?'

'Tonight, before we left. I didn't trust him!' He gave a short mirthless laugh. 'He told me you'd discouraged his attempts at flirtation. I could wish that you'd done the same tonight.'

'That was no flirtation,' she cried, her voice breaking.

Jarrod swore angrily, swinging the car round a sharp bend. 'No. You're right,' he muttered. 'It was almost something quite different!'

'Jarrod, please!' she begged. 'Don't—don't!' She put her hand over her ears, and he refused to look at her until they reached the Lodge.

Helen was waiting for them on the veranda, her face pale and drawn. She hurried down to meet them, and Sara shrank back wearily. She couldn't face Helen's piercing eyes tonight.

'Oh, Jarrod,' she was saying, 'thank God you're back! There's been a telephone call from England. J.K. has had another heart attack!'

For a moment, Jarrod said nothing, then he said quietly: 'What did they say?' He looked pale. 'Is he alive?'

Helen sighed distractedly. 'I think so. He was when the call was made, but it sounded as though it was touch and go. Oh, Jarrod, do you think he's going to die?'

Jarrod shook his head. 'Don't ask me questions I can't answer, Helen. Have you rung the airport?'

'Of course. There's a flight from Montego at midnight. I've made a provisional booking for four.'

'Four? Oh, I see. You're coming, too.'

'Yes.' Helen nodded. 'I—I must see him.'

Jarrod nodded as though he understood that, and then glanced at Sara, who was leaning against the car weakly, looking at them with horrified eyes. 'You heard?'

Sara nodded, not trusting herself to speak.

'Good. Go collect a few things. We leave in fifteen minutes.'

Sara nodded again, and hastened up the steps into the house. It was strange how J.K. had been in her thoughts all day, firstly with his card, and then later when she had wanted to telephone him.

And now he was desperately ill and they might not get there in time. It was frightening.

As she thrust her belongings carelessly into an overnight case, she thought how terrible it was that J.K. had been so ill while she and Jarrod ... She bit her lips to stop them from trembling. Was she never to stop making a fool of herself where he was concerned? Everything that had happened to her had been her own fault. How he must despise her in reality, how bitterly she regretted tormenting him, attempting to destroy his control, when now he had to face this—this tragedy, with no one to whom he could turn. Even his mother had had no deep feelings for J.K. and she, Sara, who might have shared his grief, had destroyed any small part of friendship between them.

CHAPTER TEN

SARA sat on the wide window seat of the lounge of Malthorpe Hall, staring out over the gardens with unseeing eyes. Only the rain was real, falling heavily outside, soaking the trees and lawns, dripping from the terraces in a never-ending stream. She thought it was a fitting end to a terrible day. This afternoon they had buried J.K. in the cemetery not far from the Hall, where all the squires of Malthorpe had been buried. Not that J.K. had ever been that, but he had enjoyed the same popularity in the village. She had not cried, she had not been able to cry, and her eyes were hot and burning, as though she was running a fever.

Since the terrible night of their departure from Jamaica she had had plenty of time for tears, but they had not come. In the three days J.K. survived after their arrival back in England, when the best specialists Jarrod could summon were attempting to save J.K.'s life, she had sat for long hours on this same window seat, when she was not at the hospital, sitting by J.K.'s bedside, holding his hand and loving him, willing him to live.

But it had all been to no avail. His heart was too weak, it could not stand the strain of the second attack, and they had all been so helpless, just waiting for him to die.

Helen had cried, she had been stricken with grief, and at the funeral had aroused the sympathy of everyone who had attended. It had been a big funeral, an important funeral, the little village church filled to capacity with mourners, many of whom had come from overseas to pay their last repects to a man admired and liked in business.

It was Jarrod who seemed to bear the whole weight of the awful arrangements that had to be made. Seeing him going about the Hall, driving in the Rolls, instead of in one of his fast cars, always dressed in dark suits, his face dark and withdrawn, Sara could see little resemblance to the man she had spent so many happy hours with in Jamaica, for in spite of that last evening, she remembered the good times with despairing intensity.

Her enforced solitude had given her time to think, time to consider her own future, and to make arrangements to remove the responsibility of herself from Jarrod's shoulders. It had been different when J.K. was alive, then he had been the mainstay of her existence, but now that he was dead, she had no intention of sponging on Jarrod any longer. Besides, no doubt now he would get married, and provide himself with a family, and she didn't want to be around to witness that.

So she had contacted the textile firm in Bridchester, for whom her grandfather had worked for so many years, and they had offered her a job as a trainee textile designer, a job which while being moderately paid would eventually provide her with an adequate career. For although at this moment, she loved Jarrod as she had been forced to admit to herself that she did, time might ease that partticular pain and give her a tolerable life. She doubted whether she would ever marry. There was no doubt in her mind that she would never stop loving Jarrod, but maybe the desire for children of her own might one day overcome her other objections.

The door opened, and Lauren Maxwell came in. Dressed in a slim-fitting black suit with an astrakhan collar that suited her golden colouring very well, she looked sleek and sophisticated. Beside her, Sara's pale cheeks, auburn hair and grey dress looked dull and uninteresting. She seemed pleased when she saw Sara there, and said:

'Well, it's all over. Everyone has gone, except my mother and father. I expect you're feeling pretty depressed.'

Sara nodded. 'Aren't we all?' she murmured.

Lauren gave her a speculative look. 'Some more than others, I would suppose,' she remarked sardonically, and Sara felt her nerves tighten.

'What do you mean?'

Lauren shrugged her elegant shoulders. 'Darling, don't be naïve. You know perfectly well what I mean. After all, J.K. was your surety of a meal ticket for life, wasn't he?'

Sara stared at her in horror. 'You don't imagine that was how I thought of him?' she cried.

Lauren sighed. 'Oh, spare me the histrionics, darling, I don't blame you. A working girl has to grab every opportunity that comes her way. I suppose I would have done just the same in the same circumstances. Unfortunately, Jarrod isn't quite so gullible, is he?'

Sara got to her feet jerkily. 'How dare you speak to me like this?' she exclaimed. 'My reasons for coming here were purely unmercenary ones. I don't want J.K.'s money, I never did! He wanted me here—my grandfather had made that stupid clause in his will—and J.K. practically forced me into it!'

'Oh, come on!' Lauren lounged into a chair, crossing her legs and taking out her cigarettes. 'You don't think anyone, least of all Jarrod, believes that, do you? Heavens, as I've said, you were on to a good thing. Unfortunately it didn't last long enough for you to benefit from it. I should hazard a guess that in a couple of years you could have amassed quite a small fortune, with careful consideration.'

'How can you talk this way, when J.K. has hardly had time to settle in his coffin!' exclaimed Sara, her throat dry and uncomfortable. 'I thought you liked him!'

'So I did, darling, but I liked his money even more.' She gave a short laugh. 'How gauche you sound, Sara. Sometimes I could almost believe you were for real. Did you fall off the Christmas tree or something? Or were you always so green!'

'Oh, please!' Sara put her hands over her ears. 'This is terrible! Don't say any more! Anyway, I—I shall be leaving, so that need not worry you!'

Lauren lit her cigarette, and drew deeply upon it. 'Darling, it doesn't bother me at all. It seems obvious now that Jarrod will want to settle down at last. As the eldest member of the family, he can hardly behave so carelessly, and I, as the most suitable candidate, should soon become Mrs. Jarrod Kyle.' She smiled. 'Doesn't that sound nice! Mrs. Jarrod Kyle!'

'It sounds delightful, darling,' remarked another voice, and Sara turned in astonishment to find Tracy Merrick leaning against the door post. 'My, my,

Lauren, you don't waste any time, do you? Are you already dividing up the estate into his and hers?'

Lauren rose to her feet, and the two faced each other angrily. Sara gave them a helpless look, then turned and left the room, closing the door behind her. She had not known Tracy was here. She had not attended the funeral, so Jarrod must have sent for her.

She walked towards the stairs wearily, when Jarrod appeared from the study. 'Ah, there you are, Sara,' he said detachedly. 'We're waiting for you. Mr. Winstanley is here to read the will.'

'The will!' Sara pressed a hand to her throat. 'Oh, but that's nothing to do with me!'

'Oh, but it is! All the beneficiaries are to be present. You are one of them—like it or not!'

And without giving her time to argue, he propelled her with undue haste into the study. Mr. Winstanley was there, with several of the servants, and Doctor Landry.

Sara stood near the door, refusing Jarrod's indication that she should be seated. She wanted none of this. It seemed hateful, dividing J.K.'s possessions so soon after his death. Her cheeks were pale, and she was conscious that for the first time in days Jarrod was studying her intently. Helen was not here, but Mr. Winstanley explained that she had been overcome with grief and would hear of her bequest later.

The servants were all left a substantial sum of money for their faithful service, and they filed out after their bequests were read. Then came Doctor Landry, who received a gift of ten thousand pounds, and the jade chessmen that Sara had so admired. Jarrod, of course, inherited the whole of J.K.'s estate, his controlling interest in Kyle Textiles and Malthorpe Hall. Sara was the final beneficiary, and she stiffened when Mr. Winstanley spoke her name.

'To my son's ward, Sara Robins, I bequeath my whole collection of antique porcelain and jade, my pictures and miniatures, for I know she will derive sufficient funds from their sale to live comfortably for the rest of her life.' Mr. Winstanley intoned the words solemnly, and Sara pressed the palms of her hands to her burning cheeks.

'Oh no!' she whispered, shaking her head. 'No. *No!*' She looked desperately at the solicitor. 'I can't —I can't! I don't want anything!' She glanced at Jarrod, who was watching her solemnly. 'Please, can't you see? J.K. owed me nothing—nothing at all!'

Jarrod moved. 'There is no mention of your requiring any payment,' he said briefly. 'The gift is what it is. A gift.'

Sara shook her head. 'I don't want them, I tell you,' she said, shaking her head desperately. 'Mr. Winstanley, I couldn't *sell* J.K.'s collection!'

Jarrod lifted the will from the desk. 'The collection is worth between fifty and sixty thousand pounds,' he said. 'You can sell it to me!'

Sara stared at him. 'To you?'

'Of course. That was what my father intended, I imagine.'

She continued to shake her head. 'You can have the collection! I don't want any part of it! Can't you see? I *loved* J.K.! I wish he was still here! I don't want your money!' Her voice broke off on a sob, and to her astonishment she felt tears streaming down her cheeks.

'My dear child——' began Doctor Landry, while Mr. Winstanley looked uncomfortable.

Sara looked from Mr. Winstanley to Doctor Landry, and from them to Jarrod, standing so still, looking so dear and familiar suddenly, watching her, and she couldn't bear it. There was only one thing in this room she wanted, and he didn't even realise she had feelings.

She opened the door, thrusting her way out, ignoring the surprised glances of Tracy and Lauren who were standing in the wide hall. She ran up the stairs as though the devil himself was at her heels, sobbing uncontrollably, unaware that Jarrod was following her, his face strained, his eyes anxious. But Tracy and Lauren watched this sudden action, and their faces were astounded.

Sara ran to her room, throwing open the door, closing it, leaning back against it, aching with the misery she was experiencing. Oh God, she prayed violently, make the pain go away, make it go away *soon*.

She felt the door opening behind her, and pressed against it. 'Go away, go away, whoever it is,' she cried. 'Leave me alone!'

The door was pushed powerfully, and she was almost thrown off balance as Jarrod came in, closing the door himself, staring at her with tormented eyes. 'Oh, Sara,' he muttered, 'you're a crazy idiot, do you know that?'

Then, astonishingly, astoundingly, amazingly, he pulled her into his arms, pressing her close against the hard length of his body. "This is what you wanted, isn't it?' he muttered, burying his face in her neck. 'You weren't fooling me down there, were you? What I read in your eyes was love, wasn't it?' His voice was husky with emotion, and he drew back to stare at her comprehendingly.

She wound her arms round his neck, crying and laughing at the same time. 'Oh, Jarrod,' she exclaimed, pulling his mouth to hers.

For a long while there was silence in the room. They were hungry for one another, and there was no assuaging Jarrod's emotions. At last, he drew back, pulling her down on to the bed beside him. 'Before you get anything else wrong, I love you,' he said, winding her hair round his fingers. 'But if you marry me you'll be marrying a man twice your age!'

'Are you asking me?' Sara stared at him.

'Are you accepting?'

'Oh yes, yes, yes!' Sara raised his hand to her cheek.

'But Sara, you're crazy! Why me? For me, it's different. I've been around. With you, you've your whole life ahead of you, and now you've got the means to live any kind of life you choose.'

Sara sighed disbelievingly, wiping her cheeks with the back of her hand. 'You always underestimated me,' she murmured smilingly.

'I underestimated J.K. and most of all myself, but never you,' he muttered. 'Right from the beginning, I knew you were Trouble, with a capital T.'

'You didn't like me in those days,' said Sara, frowning at the remembrance.

'I resented you,' he corrected her gently. 'Don't you know you've twisted your way into my heart right from the very beginning? There you were, a wistful waif in that awful Mason woman's house, and I knew then that you were going to live in my house, disturbing me, and I resented you for it. No woman has ever disturbed me, and I guess after my father's unsatisfactory marriage I wanted no part of that kind of relationship.'

'You always treated me as though you hated me!'

He smiled. 'Well, maybe I did! After all, nobody likes to think they're vulnerable.' He sighed. 'And then when I picked you up off the road that night you got soaking wet, I found myself wanting you.' He traced her bone structure with his finger. 'Do you know what that means? Wanting you?'

'I suppose so,' she flushed.

'It means wanting to possess you, to possess your body and mind to the exclusion of anything else. And I was used to getting what I wanted. Oh yes, I admit it. And I hated myself because you were too young!'

'Oh no!'

'Oh yes. So I stayed away, even though I wanted to see you. I knew you'd been ill, but I couldn't trust myself. Then that night when you phoned you started it all again, and I had to come. When I saw you on the landing, looking so small and defenceless; it was all I could do not to touch you—to take you.' He sighed, kissing the curve of her ear. 'I want you now, do you know that?'

Her colour deepened becomingly. 'I'm very old for you,' he muttered, and she slid her arms round his neck.

'Go on,' she said, 'tell me the rest.'

He smiled. 'All right.' He caressed her arms softly. 'Well, J.K. arranged this trip to Jamaica, and

I knew he wasn't well. Doctor Landry had warned me of that, but he was so insistent that I couldn't refuse to take you.'

'So you didn't hate me then?'

'Hate you! Oh God!' Jarrod lay on his back on the bed staring at the ceiling. 'You have no idea what it was like, particularly as you persisted in taunting me. When I kissed you on the beach I couldn't help myself any longer. If we'd stayed in Jamaica, I would have told you the truth.'

Sara looked down at him lovingly. 'Oh, Jarrod,' she murmured, 'if only I'd known. I've loved you for so long. Right from the beginning, I think.'

Jarrod kissed her once and then sat up. 'Honey, we can't stay here,' he murmured. 'But before we go, I'll tell you something else. I think J.K. wanted this to happen. I think that's why he left you the collection, because he knew you would never be sure that I believed you when you said you came here because of him, and not because of the money. This way, he has given you the chance to escape if you want to.' He stood up, and thrust his hands into his trousers pockets. 'I guess I should give you that chance, too.'

'What do you mean?' Sara felt those cold fingers gripping her heart again.

'You rang the Bridchester warehouse yesterday and were told you had been given the position as trainee designer, is that right?'

Sara nodded. 'How did you know that?'

'Arnold Radcliffe is a friend of mine. He knew who you were. That's not why he gave you the job, I might add, before you start jumping to the wrong conclusions. But he's quite prepared to give you the same position in his Paris office, and I think maybe that's what you should do.'

Sara stared at him, ice cold now. 'Jarrod!'

He turned away. 'Don't look at me like that, Sara.'

Sara shook her head incredulously. 'Jarrod, you said you loved me!' Her voice broke.

He swung round. 'I know—and I do! But can't you see how it is with me? I'm a very possessive man—what I have, I hold. You're too young to be shackled like that. I shouldn't have spoken yet!'

'Jarrod!' She pressed her hand to her throat. 'Jarrod, no!'

He bent his head. 'You're making it very hard for me,' he said unsteadily.

Sara suddenly realised her own powers over him. With an angry movement she twisted herself into his arms, pressing herself close against him.

'Now say it,' she demanded angrily. 'Now tell me I must go to Paris!'

Jarrod stiffened, and then his arms went round her, and she knew she had won. 'Oh, Sara,' he muttered, 'it's as I said. You are a witch!'

'A *Sea Witch*?' she asked impishly.

'No—a moon witch,' he answered, burying his face in her silky hair.

Your FREE gift includes

Sweet Revenge by **Anne Mather**
Devil in a Silver Room by **Violet Winspear**
Gates of Steel by **Anne Hampson**
No Quarter Asked by **Janet Dailey**

FREE Gift Certificate
and subscription reservation

Mail this coupon today!

In the U.S.A.
1440 South Priest Drive
Tempe, AZ 85281

In Canada
649 Ontario Street
Stratford, Ontario N5A 6W2

Harlequin Reader Service:

Please send me my 4 Harlequin Presents books free. Also, reserve a subscription to the 6 new Harlequin Presents novels published each month. Each month I will receive 6 new Presents novels at the low price of $1.75 each [*Total – $10.50 a month*]. There are no shipping and handling or any other hidden charges. I am free to cancel at any time, but even if I do, these first 4 books are still mine to keep absolutely FREE without any obligation.

NAME	(PLEASE PRINT)

ADDRESS

| CITY | STATE / PROV. | ZIP / POSTAL CODE |

Offer expires October 31, 1982
Offer not valid to present subscribers

BS039

Prices subject to change without notice.